Amy Cross is the author of more than 100 horror, paranormal, fantasy and thriller novels.

OTHER TITLES
BY AMY CROSS INCLUDE

American Coven
Annie's Room
The Ash House
Asylum
B&B
The Bride of Ashbyrn House
The Camera Man
The Curse of Wetherley House
The Devil, the Witch and the Whore
Devil's Briar
The Dog
Eli's Town
The Farm
The Ghost of Molly Holt
The Ghosts of Lakeforth Hotel
The Girl Who Never Came Back
Haunted
The Haunting of Blackwych Grange
The Night Girl
Other People's Bodies
Perfect Little Monsters & Other Stories
The Shades
The Soul Auction
Tenderling
Ward Z

The House on Everley Street

Death Herself book 2

AMY CROSS

First published by Dark Season Books,
United Kingdom, 2018

ISBN: 9781980698302

Also available in e-book format.

www.amycross.com

CONTENTS

AMY CROSS

THE HOUSE ON EVERLEY STREET

DEATH HERSELF BOOK 2

AMY CROSS

PROLOGUE

"DAISY!" SHE SHOUTED, hurrying through the door and racing to the cot. "What's wrong? Are you okay?"

Reaching in and scooping the crying baby up, Deborah examined her daughter's screaming face before turning and looking around the dark room. Light from the moon shone through the nursery window, casting dancing, ever-changing shadows across the far wall, but as she turned she realized that there was no sign of anything amiss. Still, Daisy's screams were loud and urgent, and Deborah turned again to look around, convinced that she was missing the cause.

"Is she okay?" Mike asked, hurrying through. "What's going on in here?"

"What do you *think's* going on in here?"

Deborah shouted at him. "It's the same as last time, but a thousand times worse!" She held the child closer, trying to calm her screams. "Come on, sweetheart," she whispered, gently rocking Daisy from side to side. "It's okay, I'm here now."

"Let's just calm down," Mike replied, taking a look at Daisy before glancing around the room. Heading over to the window, he tried to slide it open but found that it was still locked. "Nothing got in, she just... She must have had a nightmare, that's all."

"You heard the banging sound," Deborah said firmly. "Don't you dare try to deny it this time."

"Can't you get her to be quiet?"

"I'm trying!" she hissed, before kissing Daisy's forehead. "Sweetheart, please, Mummy's here now. Oh God, Mike, I think she's turning blue! She's crying so much, she's not breathing properly!"

If anything, this only caused the child to scream louder than ever as tears rolled down her flushed face.

"Maybe it was something in the garden," Mike muttered, squinting a little as he peered out. Unfastening the lock, he slid the window open and leaned over the edge. For a moment, he studied the shadows below, but once again he quickly realized there was nothing that could possibly be to blame. Just darkness and light rain. Turning, he looked around for something else, *anything* else, that could have been the source of the sudden banging sound that had woken them a moment earlier and caused their daughter to scream.

"We can't stay in this house," Deborah continued, pushing past him and carrying Daisy to the door. "I can't do this anymore!"

"Wait!" Hurrying after her, he grabbed her arm at the top of the stairs and pulled her back. "Where are you going? You can't let a few bumps in the middle of the night run us out of our own home!"

"A few bumps?" Close to tears but too angry to cry, she stared at him in dumbstruck horror, unable to believe that he was still peddling the same tired old explanations. "It's not a few bumps, Mike. It's constant, it's every night and it's driving us insane! We can't let Daisy grow up in this environment!"

"So what are you saying?" he asked. "That the house is haunted?"

"I'm saying I can't spend another night here, and neither can Daisy." She paused, frustrated by his refusal to accept the truth, before finally sighing. "I'll take her to my mother's. It's the only solution. I'll take her and we'll stay there until we can sell this house and buy another one."

"The market -"

"Screw the market!" she shouted, before

kissing the side of Daisy's head. "It's okay, sweetheart, Mummy's got you. We're not going to spend another night in this awful place. Please, try not to cry."

"If we sell now," Mike continued, "we'll lose up to -"

"I don't care!" she shouted. "If we *don't* sell now, we'll lose our minds!"

"But if we just wait another -"

Before he could finish, the door to the nursery slammed shut with sudden, violent force, before rebounding toward the wall.

"I suppose that was the wind, was it?" Deborah asked.

"I opened the window a minute ago -"

"That's the problem," she continued. "No matter what happens, you always come up with an explanation."

"Just because I don't automatically assume the worst -"

"The worst? It's the truth!" She looked down at Daisy again. "Please, sweetie, stop crying. Everything's going to be okay. You have to take deep breaths."

"There's no such thing as ghosts," Mike told her. "You never used to believe in them either."

"Not until we moved in here."

"Debbie -"

"I mean it," she said firmly, her voice

trembling as she held back tears. "There's something wrong with this place."

He sighed again.

"I'm sorry," she added, before turning and hurrying down the stairs with her crying daughter still in her arms. "We're getting out of here," she continued, kissing the top of Daisy's head as she ran to the hallway, grabbed the car keys and then pulled the door open.

Rain was still falling outside but she didn't care, not as she raced barefoot across the gravel driveway and hurriedly opened one of the car's rear doors. Leaning in, she began to strap Daisy into the child-seat.

"It's going to be okay," she explained, hoping against hope that her daughter would stop crying now that they were out of the house. "We should have left weeks ago, but at least we're getting out of here now."

"Wait!" Mike shouted, hurrying after her. "You're being irrational!"

"You didn't hear it!" she replied, turning to him as rain fell all around them. "You didn't hear it talking to her!"

"Debbie -"

"Don't tell me I imagined it!"

"Did you ever actually see anything?" he asked.

"I felt it!" she shouted. "There's something

in there!"

"Debbie -"

"Don't you dare!" she hissed, before looking back toward the house. A light was still on in one of the bedrooms, but apart from that the house was shrouded in darkness, with rain falling faster and harder with each passing second. "It was whispering to her. I heard its voice in there, saying the most awful things. I thought I heard it before, but I was never sure, not until tonight, but it's real." She turned back to him. "I know this sounds insane, and I know you probably think I'm losing my mind, but... Are you seriously telling me that you can't feel that *thing*, whatever it is?"

"Debbie -"

"When you're alone in the house," she continued breathlessly, as she moved strands of wet hair from across her face, "do you ever really feel *truly* alone? Or do you feel that presence, whatever it is, constantly with you? Like there's something in there, another soul." She waited for an answer. "Be honest, Mike. Don't tell me what you think you should be feeling, tell me what's actually in your heart. Forget about explanations for now and just focus on what's happening. Do you really think we can continue to live in that house?"

He opened his mouth to reply, before looking down and seeing Daisy still crying in her seat.

"She's probably damaged already," Deborah added. "Please, for all our sakes, let's just go."

"I.."

He paused, still watching Daisy.

"Get in and wait for me," he said finally, pulling the driver's door open. "I'll go back inside and grab a few things, and then, fine, we'll go to your mother's. We can come up with another plan tomorrow, we can work something out, but you're right."

"You feel it too, don't you?"

"I feel... something. Whatever's in the house, *if* there's something in there, I'm not going to let it hurt our daughter." With that, he leaned forward and kissed Deborah on the cheek before turning and hurrying back inside.

"Be careful!" she called after him, before getting into the car. Soaking wet and out of breath, she turned and smiled at Daisy, who was still screaming as loud as she could manage. "It's okay, sweetheart. We're going, do you see? We're leaving this house and we're never, ever going to have to come back. Mummy promises." Reaching out, she used a trembling hand to wipe some of the rain from the girl's bawling face. "I don't know what you saw in your nursery, but I swear to God, I won't let it affect you. If you need help, we'll get it. Maybe you won't even remember this, but if you do, I promise everything'll be okay." Spotting movement nearby, she turned just in time to see Mike pulling the front door of the house shut and then hurrying to the car with a hold-all over his shoulder.

"It's all locked up," he said as soon as he was in the passenger seat. Pulling the door shut, he turned to her. "I swear to God, Debbie, until tonight I never would have believed it was possible."

"But you believe it now, don't you? Please tell me you don't think I'm losing my mind."

"I don't think you're losing your mind," he replied, staring straight ahead. Beyond the rain-soaked windshield, the dark house stood in brooding silence, as if it was waiting for them to change their minds and go back inside. "I think there really *is* something in there."

"Where do you feel it most?" she asked.

"I... I don't know."

"Sometimes in the kitchen," she continued, watching the house's dark upstairs windows, "I feel like I can almost hear it. Only almost, though. It's like it's on the very edge of my perception."

Mike nodded. "I know."

"Maybe we can get our money back," she suggested. "No-one told us the place was haunted when we bought it, maybe legally we can force them to take the place back. Isn't there some rule that you have to inform potential buyers of this kind of thing?"

"I'm not sure the law's really set up to take

ghosts into account," he replied, "but we'll see. If we can't do that, we'll sell it. Whatever happens, we'll find somewhere else to live, because I swear..." He paused, staring out at the house for a moment longer, and feeling as if in some strange way it was staring right back at him. "I am never going back into number one, Everley Street, again. If it wasn't for the money, I'd burn the place down right now."

Putting the key into the ignition, Deborah started the car and began to reverse out of the driveway, with Daisy still crying.

"You don't think it's scarred her for life, do you?" she asked, stopping the car and then turning the wheel before hitting the accelerator. "What if it's done permanent damage?"

"No chance," he replied as they drove away. "Everything'll be okay. I promise you, honey, I promise both of you. We're not going to let that house destroy us. We got out in time." He turned to Daisy, who was still screaming. "Jesus Christ, is she never going to stop? We have to get her to the hospital! I don't think she's breathing properly, she's starting to get blue lips!"

"Wait, is she -"

"Just hurry!" he shouted, climbing to the back seat. "Take us to the hospital! I'm going to try to get her to stop crying so she can breathe!"

As the car screeched off into the night, the

house on Everley Street stood silently in the torrential rain, with all the lights off and all the exterior doors locked. From the outside, the rush of rain was overwhelming; from the inside, there was a steady pitter-patter on the windows, but for the most part the rest of the house was completely quiet. Out on the landing, however, there was the faintest sound of a whisper coming from somewhere within the house, and a moment later the nursery's door swung slowly shut.

CHAPTER ONE

Today

"I GUESS YOU'RE THE EXPERT WHEN IT COMES TO GHOSTS."

John turned to him, momentarily thrown. "I am?"

"The big writer and all." Smiling, Aaron stepped out onto the balcony, away from the party. A cool night breeze ruffled his hair as he made his way to the edge and looked out across the vast, starry city. "The man who knows how to really scare people. I must say, I thought it was a good wheeze to put an actual medical warning on the cover of your new book. I'm sure that'll shift a few more copies. That and the reassuring message about blaming one's parents for all of one's unfortunate experiences."

John frowned. "That's not the message at all."

"Are you sure? I finished it last night. Your protagonist basically suffers throughout his life due to having been raised by sadists. He blames them for everything."

"He doesn't blame them. He fights back, but their influence is too strong."

"Either way," Aaron said with a grin, "I don't want to fight. I'm sure it'll be a hit."

"Maybe." John paused, turning to look back at the crowd of people in the penthouse's main room. He hated book launches at the best of times, especially his own, but this one felt even more sickly than usual. He kept expecting something to go catastrophically wrong, as if some hidden danger was lurking just out of sight. This wasn't exactly a new sensation, in fact it was one he lived with all the time, but tonight it felt particularly strong. After a moment, he made eye contact with his wife Sarah, and she smiled at him before continuing her conversation with some minor C-list actor. Unlike John, Sarah knew exactly how to schmooze people. She was, in all respects, his better half.

"How many people live in London again?" Aaron asked, nudging his arm. "Five million? Six?"

"Something like that," John replied, turning to look out at the city. "Too many."

"Misanthrope. How many would you prefer?"

"One or two million would be about right. Then the place wouldn't be so crowded."

"And how many ghosts do you think there are?"

John opened his mouth to reply, but the words caught. "I have no idea," he said finally.

"But there must be billions, mustn't there? If everyone who ever died is still floating about, where are they? If they're real, why don't we ever get a glimpse of them?"

"I have no idea," John said with a faint smile. "I don't really go into the science of it too much. I just make things up for a living, remember?"

"But don't you think it's kind of juvenile?" Aaron continued, leaning against the railing and looking down at the busy street far below. A coach was just pulling away from the front of the hotel, joining the sea of lights that criss-crossed the city. "What's the difference between believing in ghost and believing in... fairies? Or leprechauns? Hell, even unicorns! Aren't you basically a writer of fairy-tales?"

At this, John allowed himself another smile.

"What's wrong?" Aaron asked. "Not macho enough for you?"

"I just don't know where to begin proving

you wrong," John replied, before wincing slightly as he heard someone guffawing with laughter nearby. He hated that about himself, the fact that he got so tense around loud people, and he was tempted to tell the next interviewer that the increasing gap between each book was entirely down to the fact that he loathed publicity events. He felt certain he could write faster, maybe even better, if people left him alone.

"Jesus," Aaron continued, "we have this same conversation every year, don't we?"

"More or less," John said quietly, sipping from his wine glass. "Every book launch, at least."

"And I guess I shouldn't have the temerity to challenge you on this subject. Like I said, you *are* the expert. If you say ghosts are real, then I suppose I must just take it at face value."

"Did I say they're real?" John asked.

"More or less."

"I'm not sure about that."

"You couldn't write about them so convincingly if you had doubts," Aaron told him.

John smiled again, but he knew full well that Aaron was watching him intently. Every single time the pair of them met up, John ended up feeling as if he was under attack. Aaron had a tendency to enjoy chipping away at the beliefs of his friends, but whereas John had once enjoyed these discussions, now he was starting to tire of the whole thing. Truth be told, he felt he was getting a little sick of Aaron altogether, but he could never truly acknowledge that fact. After all, Aaron was by far his closest friend.

"You never answered my question," Aaron said finally.

"What question is that?"

"You know the one. The one you avoid every time we talk."

"Some people might take that as a hint."

"Not me."

"Evidently not."

There was a pause. John knew what was coming next.

"So," Aaron said finally, "*have* you ever seen a ghost? I mean, for a guy who's made a billion-dollar career as the world's most successful horror novelist, it'd be kind of disingenuous if you hadn't had at least one spooky encounter. Something to fire the creative juices?"

John stared out at the late-night city vista for a moment. "Tell me what you see," he said finally.

"Out there?" Aaron turned to look. "Not much. A lot of lights."

"Exactly," John replied. "Your gaze is drawn to the lights, mine is drawn to the darkness. How many people do you think are being murdered in this city right now?"

Aaron sighed.

"How many are being raped? Robbed? Emotionally abused?" Warming to his theme, John almost didn't notice his phone vibrating in his pocket, but finally he slipped it out. "How many people are sobbing in absolute despair? How many are holding a knife to their wrist?"

"Morbid, much?" Aaron asked.

"I've got to take this," John said, grinning, before he'd even checked to see who was calling. "It might be my agent." Glancing at the screen, he saw he was almost right: it was his lawyer.

"When you're done," Aaron replied, "I want a definitive answer to my question. Have you, the great John Myers, ever seen a ghost?"

"Hey," John said, answering the call and turning to wander back across the terrace. He smiled briefly at Sarah and she smiled back at him, but he made his way past the door to the penthouse and around the side, across to the darker part of the outside area. "You just saved my ass," he continued, taking a sip from his glass. "I was actually thinking about jumping, that's how dull this whole event is. What's up?"

"You asked me to call," Reginald said, on the other end of the line, "if the house on Everley Street ever came on the market."

"Sure, why -" John stopped suddenly, feeling a faint shiver run up his back. "And has it?"

"I just got an alert. It was put up about two

hours ago, the price tag is -"

"I don't care what the price is," John said quickly. "Buy it."

"Well, I -"

"Contact the owners," he continued, "and offer them whatever they're asking. If they hesitate, double it. Whatever, just get it done."

"As your lawyer, I have to tell you that's not a very good negotiating tactic. We need to go in low -"

"Just get the damn house bought," John said firmly, glancing over his shoulder and seeing that Aaron was watching from a distance, well out of earshot. "Do it," he continued, turning and heading to the farthest end of the terrace, which happened to be shrouded in darkness. The city's distant lights seemed brighter now, and the stars above dimmer.

"I really don't think there's any need to move so fast," Reginald continued. "It's an ordinary, end-of-row family house on a dull little street in a dull little town. I'm sure we can haggle the price down, you'll probably be the only one who's interested anyway."

"I just want it done," he replied. "Call me when the deal's complete. I'll be here for the next couple of hours, then I've got some infernal book signing in the morning."

"You want me to conclude a deal for the house in the next couple of hours?"

"Ideally."

"John, what is it about this house on Everley Street that -"

"I'm not here to answer questions," John snapped, before realizing that he was perhaps being a little too harsh. After all, if Aaron was the closest thing he had to a friend, then Reginald was the second closest, forming an unlikely and fragile club of just two. "Reginald, please, I told you years ago that this house is important to me. I've been waiting for it to come onto the market and there's no way I'm going to miss the opportunity. I usually bow to your advice, but this time I can't wait. Buy the damn house."

Reginald sighed on the other end of the line. "You're the client, your wish is my command. If you want to throw a quarter of a million on a podgy little house that's barely worth half that, I can't stop you."

"No," John said firmly, "you can't. Sorry, I don't mean to be harsh, just..." He paused, feeling as if the whole world had suddenly shifted slightly on its axis, as if some long-forgotten thought was stirring in the back of his mind. "Let me know when the deal's done."

"Will do, boss. Over and out."

"Wait," he added, "Reginald... Do you happen to know *why* the current owners are selling?"

"I do not."

He paused. "Try to find out. Don't make a thing of it, but try to bring it up in conversation."

"Just to satisfy your curiosity?"

"Just to satisfy my curiosity."

"And you're going to tell me what this is all about one day? What does this house mean to you, anyway?"

John paused again, watching as a light crossed the horizon. Plane? Shooting star? UFO? He didn't know and he didn't care. Whatever it was, it was undoubtedly something mundane.

"Just buy the damn house," he said finally, before cutting the call. Taking a deep breath, he realized his chest felt tight, and he chose to walk the long way back around the edge of the terrace, hoping to regather his composure by the time he reached the others. He knew Aaron was still watching him, so he made his way to the door that led inside, and he signaled for Sarah to meet him. She excused herself from whoever she was talking to and made her way over to him. As ever, she seemed totally in control of the situation, as graceful and sociable as he was mannered and stiff.

"Hey," he said, trying to seem relaxed, "I'm going to be heading down to Dorset for a few days."

She frowned. "Dorset? Why?"

"Something's come up."

"In Dorset?" She smiled. "I didn't think

anything *ever* came up in Dorset."

"I just need to do something," he told her. "It's... old family stuff, that's all."

"Family stuff? Well now I know you're lying."

"It's nothing," he replied, trying not to sigh. He was already aware that he should have waited, maybe seemed more casual, but he figured there was no going back now. "I just have to take care of some business. I'd invite you, but it's going to be incredibly boring and, well, I'll tell you about it when I get back. I'll be gone a day or two, maximum."

"So you're shooting off just as the kids' school breaks up for summer holidays?"

"I'll make it up to you."

She stared at him for a moment, before slowly nodding. "Okay. I know better than to try to stop you, or to ask too many questions. You're entering one of your semi-regular mysterious phases, aren't you? The ones I tolerate because I know you'll spring back to your usual self eventually?"

"Am I really like that?"

She nodded.

"When I get back," he continued, "we'll -"

"Don't make promises," she replied, leaning closer and kissing him on the cheek. "We both know how those usually end up. Just stay safe and don't be away for more than two nights. The kids are always at their most energetic at the start of their summer holiday, you know."

"I'll make it up to you," he said again.

"Of course you will," she said, taking a step back, "and now I have to go and schmooze the editors, reviewers and media personalities *you're* supposed to be schmoozing, while you drink wine and talk to Aaron about ghosts. Come back soon, okay?"

"I haven't even left yet."

"Haven't you?" She paused, before smiling and heading back inside.

"What's that supposed to mean?" he called after her, but it was too late. She was already talking to someone he vaguely recognized from the papers. Someone who'd married someone who'd once been on a reality TV show. Nearby, on a table, dozens of copies of his new book were waiting for guests to admire

"So are you finally going to answer my question?" Aaron asked suddenly, stepping up behind him. "Have you, famous horror novelist John Myers, ever seen an actual ghost?"

John paused, before turning to look at him. "Not yet," he said after a moment, forcing a smile. "You never know, though. There's still time."

CHAPTER TWO

Twenty years ago

"WHAT ARE YOU DOING?"

Hearing his grandmother's voice in the hallway, John immediately slipped his notebook out of sight and pretended to be reading a magazine. He kept his eyes fixed firmly on the page, even as he heard his grandmother shuffling closer. A moment later, she snatched the magazine from his hands and took a look at the cover.

"What are you reading about television shows for?" she asked haughtily, clearly not approving of the subject matter. "What have television shows got to do with anything?"

"I just -"

"You should be reading about proper

things," she continued, flicking through the magazine. "Cultural things, things that'll improve your mind. This is just garbage."

"It's -"

"You're going to end up with a soft brain," she added, dropping the magazine into his lap before turning and making her way slowly to the sideboard. She was in her nightgown, ready for bed, which was always when she seemed most uppity. "You'll end up like your mother, achieving nothing in life and wasting all your potential. You're directing your energies in all the wrong directions."

"Mum didn't waste her potential," he replied, watching as his grandmother's trembling hands unscrewed the lid on the sherry bottle. "If she hadn't died, she'd have been a writer."

At this, his grandmother gave a derisory laugh.

"It's true," John continued. "Dad said she won competitions in magazines. He said she was working on something and that one day she'd get published."

"Rubbish," the old woman hissed. "Your mother had all these fancy ideas, but she was never going to get anywhere with them, she'd never have finished that stupid book, even if she'd lived to be a hundred. No wonder she ended up weak in the head. I did everything I could for her, I tried to put her on the straight and narrow, but sometimes you just can't help someone. Some people are just doomed to failure on account of their own personalities."

"She was -"

"Do you want to end up like her? Locking yourself in the bathroom and downing a bottle of bleach?"

John shivered a little as he heard those words. Looking back down at the magazine, he suddenly felt a little hollow, as if his grandmother's words had struck at his core. Any mention of his mother's suicide was always enough to knock him off kilter.

"You're lucky you were too young to remember," she continued. "*I* remember. Course I do, I'm the poor soul who had to hear the screams and break down the door. I'll never forget the moment I saw her writhing in agony on the floor with blood pouring from her mouth, while you cried in your room. That's the problem with suicides, they're so selfish, they never think about the people who have to find them."

"Mum wasn't selfish," John said quietly.

"What was that?" she asked, raising her voice. "What did you say?"

"Nothing."

"Did you say she wasn't selfish? What do you know, eh? She was weak and pathetic, and rather than buckling down to a proper life, she decided to take the easy way out." Finishing the glass of sherry, she poured herself a second. "You don't know what you're talking about. You don't even remember your mother."

"I do," he replied, a little defensively. "I mean, I remember... flashes. I remember what she looked like."

"Lucky you."

"And I remember the sound of her voice."

"She was always a whiner."

"She had a lot of self doubt," John continued. "I remember -"

"You don't remember anything."

"But -"

"You were just a child when she died," she added, interrupting him as she took another sip of sherry. "It's impossible for you to remember anything about her at all, but if you did, you'd know what a mess she was. She used to cry at the drop of a pin, she never had the strength to be anything in life. I'm telling you, you're lucky she cleared herself out of the way. If she'd raised you, you'd be an insufferable wimp. She'd have been a malignant influence. Fortunately, you've got me now to make sure you grow a spine."

He opened his mouth to reply, to insist that he *did* remember his mother, but at the last moment he held back. He'd learned long ago that there was no point arguing with his grandmother. She often got drunk and ranted about the past, and he knew she was incapable of admitting she was wrong. All he could do was let her say whatever she wanted and then go to bed, leaving her to drink alone. On a good night, that would be enough.

**

A few hours later, sitting by himself on his bed, he leafed through some more of the old handwritten pages from his mother's tin. His mother had been a keen short story writer, and although most of her work had been thrown away following her death, he'd managed to salvage a few of the short stories and now, once again, he was reading them late at night. Even just holding the pieces of paper were enough to make him feel closer to her.

"I wrote these for you," he remembered her telling him once. "They're nothing special, I just thought they'd make you laugh."

"Can I write stories one day?" he'd asked.

"Of course you can. Anyone can, if they work at it."

He couldn't help but smile as he turned to another of the pages and found one of the little pen sketches she'd added to this particular story. They were all he had left of her; there were no photos, no videos, no recordings, none of her possessions. His grandmother had thrown everything out many years earlier, even before the funeral, but somehow he'd been able to hang on to these few stories, and he kept them carefully hidden. Even now, reading them for what must have been the thousandth time, he felt as if they offered one last connection to the past. He knew ghosts didn't exist, but a part of his mother lingered in the stories she'd written. The craziest part was that as he read those stories over and over, he still couldn't find any hint of the sadness that had caused her to take her own life.

"You can be anything you want to be," she'd told him once, just a few weeks before she'd committed suicide. "Don't let anyone tell you any different."

"What if I want to be a train driver? Or an astronaut?"

"Then go for it. I can't wait to see what you do with your life."

She'd always talked about the future with excitement, like someone who fully expected to see what came next. And yet, somehow, she'd ended up drinking bleach on the bathroom floor, as if all her optimism and hope had suddenly burst one day and left her with nothing but despair. Sometimes, he even found himself wondering whether -

"What have you got there?" his grandmother asked suddenly.

"Nothing." Panicking, he shoved the papers back into the tin, but he could already hear her stomping closer. A moment later she reached down and grabbed the tin from his hands. "It's nothing!" he blurted out. "It's mine!"

"Let me see." Pulling the lid off, she reached inside and pulled out the papers. "Stories?" she muttered. "This is your mother's handwriting!"

"It's just -"

"I thought we burned all of these."

"I -"

Before he could finish, she grabbed him by the collar and pushed him forward, slamming him face-first into the wall.

"Well," she said as he recovered, "there's no time like the present. If we missed a few, we'll get rid of them now, won't we?"

"But -"

"And we'll talk about this later," she added, with a hint of anger in her voice as she crumpled the papers in her fist and then dropped them back into the tin. "I told you not to keep things from me, my boy, and I warned you there'd be consequences if you disobeyed me."

"Wait!" he replied, reaching out and trying to grab the tin. "Can't I just have a few of them?"

"It's these stories that got her into trouble," his grandmother said firmly. "She wasted so much of her time writing them, with her head up in the clouds, she never bothered to do anything else. I told her, I warned her, I even threw them out whenever I got the chance, but she wouldn't stop!

That's what happens when you don't listen to advice from people who know better, you end up making mistakes and wasting away. By the end, the only decent thing she could do was get herself out of everyone's way."

"Please let me keep the stories," he said as she headed out to the landing. "It's just a few pieces of paper, what does it matter?"

Hurrying after her, he tried again to grab the tin, even as his grandmother made her way unsteadily down the stairs.

"You're starting to remind me of her," she muttered, swaying slightly as she reached the hallway and headed to the back door. "I've worked so hard to get rid of her influence on you, but it just keeps showing through like weeds in the garden. Sometimes I think you actually *want* to be like her."

"I just want the stories."

"What's wrong? Haven't you read them already?"

"Of course, but -"

"Then you don't need to read them again, do you?" Opening the door, she stepped out into the dark garden and set the tin on the ground. A moment later, she reached down with a cigarette lighter and set fire to one of the pieces of crumpled paper.

"No!" John shouted.

"Don't you dare disobey me!" she hissed,

pushing him back and then looking down at the tin as the flames quickly spread. "This had better be the last of them. If I find that you've been keeping anything else hidden from me, boy, there will be consequences. It's not often that you make me angry, but by jove you've disappointed me tonight. It's as if you don't appreciate anything I do for you."

"But the..." Staring at the flames, he realized it was too late to save the pages. "That was all of them," he continued, with a sense of sorrow in his chest. "That was all I had."

"And why should I believe you?" she asked, turning to him as the light from the fire caught her features. "You've already shown that you're more than willing to deceive me. I put my whole life aside to take you in, and this is how you repay me. With lies and deceit."

He shook his head, unable to stop looking at the tin. The flames were already dying down, having burned through the pages in less than a minute. There'd only be ash left, and although he knew that he could write down most of the stories from memory, he also knew that there'd be little point doing so if he was no longer able to read them in his mother's handwriting. They were gone.

"Go to your room and wait for me," his grandmother said after a moment.

He turned to her. "Please -"

"Go to your room," she said firmly, "and

wait for me. Don't make me tell you again. I'm exhausted enough already."

He knew exactly what was coming, but at the same time he also knew there was no point trying to argue with her. Heading back into the house and then upstairs, he'd already removed his shirt by the time he reached his room, and he got down onto his knees and leaned forward against the bed. Waiting, he heard his grandmother moving about in the kitchen below, getting everything ready, and finally he heard her feet on the stairs as she slowly made her way up to him. He didn't even turn to look as he heard her entering the room. He simply waited, listening to the sound of her labored breathing and contemplating the pain he was about to endure. Still, he'd always known this was the price to be paid for disobedience, so he figured he only had himself to blame.

"She used to burn me sometimes," he remembered his mother whispering one night, long ago. "Only when I was bad, though. It was always my fault. Just be good, and she'll never do it to you. You can be good, can't you?"

"I promise," he'd told her.

He'd been wrong.

"I hope you know this gives me no pleasure," his grandmother said after a moment. Even without looking, he could tell she was already smoking the cigarette she was going to use. "I'd much rather have a smart grandson, an honest grandson, but you're a filthy little liar, just like your mother. If you're not careful, you'll end up the same way as her. Is that what you want, eh?" She paused. "Still, you're young, there's time to beat it out of you. You're lucky you've got me to put you on the straight and narrow. Or do you want to be like your mother?"

"No," he whispered. It was a lie, but he knew it was the right answer.

He waited, and now that she was silent he realized it was about to happen. She was most likely choosing her spot and savoring the anticipation. Even though she always said she didn't enjoy what she did to him, he felt certain she was lying.

Suddenly he felt the cigarette's tip pressing against his back, just below his left shoulder-blade. He gasped and leaned forward, gripping the sides of the bed as he held his breath. The cigarette was still burning, and several more seconds passed before he felt it being pulled away. He took a series of sharp, deep breaths, trying to fight the agony. He knew that even the faintest cry would anger his grandmother further and cause the punishment to last longer, but the pain was intense and he had to bite his lip and hold his breath again as he squeezed his eyes tight shut. Finally, slowly, he began to feel a little strength returning.

"Hurts, doesn't it?" his grandmother

muttered.

Opening his eyes, he realized she was about to strike again.

As soon as the tip burned into his flesh for a second time, this time at the small of his back, he let out a brief, involuntary cry. Squeezing his eyes tight shut, he tried to think of his mother's stories, but when that didn't work he started to think instead about the future, about finding a way to get out of the house and away from his grandmother's punishments. All he wanted was to live a life where he wouldn't be punished for every small infraction, but at the same time he knew that these impulses were probably wrong. After all, his mother had been the same, and she'd ended up dead on the bathroom floor in their old house, with half a bottle of bleach having been poured down her throat by her own hand. If his instincts were going to lead him the same way, he supposed he should be grateful that his grandmother was around to help him. She always told him he'd thank her one day, and now he figured that maybe she was right.

One day.

"What are you?" his grandmother asked after a moment, pulling the cigarette away from John's burned back.

"Weak," he whispered, as he tensed for the next touch.

"What was your mother?"

He paused, with tears in his eyes. "Weak."

"And what will I not let you be?"

"Weak."

"You will either grow up strong," she continued, "or so help me God I won't let you grow up at all."

This time, when she pressed the cigarette against his back and began to sear his flesh, he couldn't help himself. He let out a loud cry of pain. For that reason, among others, his punishment continued for another hour, well into the night.

CHAPTER THREE

Today

"ARE YOU... ARE YOU JOHN MYERS?"

Looking up from his fried breakfast, John saw that the girl from the counter, the same girl who'd taken his order a few minutes ago and who had been conspicuously gawking at him ever since, was now loitering nervously at the other end of the table. It had obviously taken her quite some time to pluck up the courage to make an approach.

"Um..." John paused, before realizing that there was no point denying anything. Despite his best efforts over the years, his face had been plastered all over the back pages of his books. "Yes, I am."

"Oh my God," the girl continued, taking a

book and pen from her pocket and setting them on the table. The book, by some rather unbelievable coincidence, just happened to be one of John's more obscure novels, *The Beast From the Georgian Swamp*. "Like, seriously, *oh my God*! I'm a huge fan of your books, I've been reading them since I was, like, seven or eight years old. I've read every single one of them, even the bad ones!"

"Thank you," he replied with a frown.

"I always knew you grew up round here," she continued, "but I thought I read that you, like, never came back. Like, dark memories or something."

"I don't come back," he replied, wanting nothing more than to get back to his breakfast. He always found fan encounters deeply uncomfortable, but he also knew that in the twenty-first century a wrong word could easily be tweeted around the globe. "This is the first time I've been back for a number of years."

"Getting nostalgic, huh?"

"Well -"

"Or are you researching a new book?"

"I -"

"That'd be so cool," she continued. "Like, writing a book set in the town where you grew up, that'd be amazing!"

"Um -"

"Then again, I guess you don't need

someone like me telling you what'd be good for your next book. I bet you've got ideas, like, stuffed in all your drawers!"

He paused, not really sure how to answer.

"Could you..." The girl paused, before sliding the book toward him. "Could I have your autograph? I swear, I just happened to be reading this behind the counter today, it's like fate brought you here. I know that probably seems unlikely, but how else do you wanna explain it?"

"Sure," John muttered, grabbing the book and pen before quickly scribbling his name. "You want me to make it out to anyone in particular?"

"Hannah. My name's Hannah. And don't worry, you won't see it for sale online. I'm going to keep that copy forever and ever."

"Hannah." He added a few more words, before sliding the book back to her and remembering to smile. "Hi, Gary. Nice to meet you."

"So have you got any new books coming soon?" she asked, with a big, excited grin plastered across her face. "It's just, according to your website there's nothing due after *The Curse of Satan's Claws*, and a few of us were talking and wondering whether you're gonna leave, like, another big gap between books. 'Cause, you know, it's not like anyone wants to pressure you, but in these gaps between publication, we have to reread your old books and watch the movies that get made. Which suck, by the way. Almost all of them."

"I'm working on something," John replied.

"Another horror novel?"

"Another horror novel."

"Awesome, and..." She paused, before laughing nervously. "Sorry, I don't mean to act like a complete idiot, I'm just completely freaked out by this. No-one famous *ever* comes into this dumb little place, they can all afford way better food. Trust me, you do *not* want to know what's in those sausages you just ate."

John looked down at his plate. He'd eaten the sausages first, since they'd tasted so good.

"Everyone said you were too big now to ever come back to Bournemouth," Hannah continued. "They said you just spend all your time in, like, London or abroad. Not that that's a bad thing, obviously. I mean, you're, like, rich enough to do whatever you want, I guess. I know the people from the local book festival tried to get you down a heap of times and you were unavailable or something, but I also know you're famous for not really liking public appearances, so I totally get it."

"I've been very lucky."

"Actually," she added, "people kinda said you hated Bournemouth."

"Hate's a very strong word," John replied, hoping that the girl would take the hint and leave him alone. "I grew up here, I barely left until I was eighteen years old, and the world's a big place. I'd like to see as much of it as possible, and unfortunately that doesn't leave much time for retreading old ground."

"And you don't have any family round here anymore?"

He paused, feeling a little more uncomfortable. "No," he said finally. "No family."

"So have you been to the set of the movie version of *The Claws of Satan's Bride*?" she asked, clearly happy to spin rapidly from one topic to the next. "I heard Todd Wilkins is playing Karl, that sounds like the best casting ever! A few of us were talking, and we figured that Noelle Simmons would make the perfect Adrienne."

"I haven't been to the set, no," John replied. "I don't really do that kind of thing. Film sets are pretty much the most boring places on the planet, usually, especially for writers."

"Huh."

"Yeah. Huh."

John waited, but he was starting to feel that his new friend wasn't going to go away any time soon. Fortunately, a moment later the cafe's door opened and a couple of new customers entered, although Hannah didn't immediately rush to help them and actually seemed a little starstruck.

"Maybe you're needed over there," John

pointed out, gesturing toward the counter.

"What?"

He nodded toward the customers.

She turned. "Oh. Sure, I'll... Yeah." She turned to go.

John breathed a sigh of relief.

"Oh," Hannah added, turning back to him and pulling a leaflet from her pocket, "I know it's a bit of a stretch, but I figured maybe you'd be interested in this."

John sighed as he saw that the leaflet was for some kind of sci-fi reading group.

"We meet on the first Tuesday of each month," Hannah explained, her eyes glistening with excitement, "which just so happens to be tomorrow. Serendipity, huh? I always carry a few leaflets with me during my shifts, in case I meet someone who might be cool enough to want to come. If you'd be willing to stop by our humble group and say a few words, and maybe record something for our next podcast, that would be amazing. I think I speak for the whole of the group when I say that we'd literally die."

"I..." Pausing, John realized that telling the truth might not be the fastest way to get left alone. "I will certainly try to show up," he said finally, making a show of folding the leaflet and slipping it into his pocket. "No promises, though."

"Cool," Hannah said, taking a few steps

back. "Totally, amazingly cool."

Finally left alone to finish his breakfast, John took a couple more mouthfuls before stopping again as he realized his stomach was twisting in knots. He knew he was just delaying things, and after a moment he reached into his pocket and took out the front-door key he'd picked up from the estate agent's office just half an hour earlier. Turning the key around between his fingers, he realized it wasn't the same as the key he remembered using twenty years ago, but then he assumed the house had probably changed a lot in that time. He also assumed that other owners would have made a lot of alterations in the meantime. Most likely, there was very little of the old house remaining.

Still, it was time to stop making assumptions. Despite the sense of nausea in his belly, he knew it was time to go and see the place.

CHAPTER FOUR

Twenty years ago

OPENING HIS EYES SUDDENLY, he realized the phone next to the bed was ringing.

He sat up, a little startled, and saw that it was a couple of minutes before 8am. Sighing, he realized that the only people who ever called so early were his grandmother's friends. For some reason, old people just seemed to get up at the crack of dawn, and they always seemed to assume that everyone else was the same. Crawling across to the other side of the double bed that had once been his mother's, he was about to take the receiver from the cradle when he realized he *could* just let it ring. Whoever was on the other end and whatever they wanted, it was guaranteed not to be urgent.

He waited, listening in case his grandmother was downstairs, and then the phone fell silent.

"Thank God," he muttered.

Falling back down onto the bed, he winced a little as he felt the burn marks on his back. He'd become so used to them, he barely even noticed the pain anymore. Taking a deep breath, he lay and listened for a moment to the silence of the house. He knew his grandmother would be up and about already, and by 8am she could be out in the garden or even off at the supermarket. She always let him sleep in, though; she said he was a growing boy and that he needed his rest, which he figured was true enough. At just eighteen years old, he was supposed to be taking a gap year before going to university, although so far all he'd done over the summer was lounge about, read a lot of books, try writing several novels, and occasionally look at websites showing what other, more normal teenagers did with their time.

Not many of them, it turned out, spent all day, every day at home with their grandmother. Looking over at the wardrobe, he thought of the spot where he'd kept the tin with his mother's writing. The spot was empty now, and he felt the same sense of emptiness in his chest.

Suddenly the phone started ringing again. Figuring that it must be Dorothy, who never gave up until someone answered, he grabbed the receiver and lifted it from the cradle. Resistance was futile.

"Hello?" he said wearily.

"Good morning," Dorothy said, sounding bright and perky, "and how are you this fine morning, Jonathan?"

"Fine, thank you Mrs. Ormerey. Do you want to speak to my grandmother?"

"If it's not too much trouble, dear."

"I'll see if she's in."

Setting the receiver down, he hauled himself out of bed and grabbed a towel, wrapping it around his waist before heading to the door and leaning out to the landing. He waited, hearing nothing but silence, but although his first reaction was to assume that his grandmother was out of the house, there was a faint, flickering doubt in his chest. Something just seemed to be tugging at his senses, and whispering in his ear that although the house *was* silent, it was a different kind of silence compared to other mornings. He turned and looked back at the phone for a moment, before stepping out onto the landing and heading to the top of the stairs.

"Gran?" he called out.

No reply.

Silence.

But still... The wrong type of silence, the type that seemed poised to surprise. It was as if the entire house was holding its breath.

He looked toward the bathroom, but the door

was open and there was no sound coming from within. Making his way toward the window, he looked out at the garden, but even though the sun was shining and there was only a gentle breeze, his grandmother was nowhere to be seen. Plus, the greenhouse door was shut, which was never the case if the old woman was pottering about out there. He glanced along at her bedroom door and saw that it was slightly ajar, which was unusual since she always kept it closed when she was in there and wide open when she wasn't, so he made his way over to check, rubbing the back of his neck in the process. He figured old Dorothy could just wait a little while longer, and that maybe she'd learn not to call so goddamn early.

Pushing the door open, he saw his grandmother sitting on the floor, with her back against the wall.

"Gran?" he said with a frown.

He waited.

No reply.

"Gran?"

Silence. Louder silence than before.

He took a step forward. The old woman's eyes were shut and she looked to be unconscious, while her bed was ruffled and had clearly been slept in. Still, considering her arthritis and osteoporosis, the sight of her on the floor was somewhat startling. Reaching down, he nudged her shoulder.

"Gran?"

Again, he waited.

Not even a twitch.

Slowly, in the pit of his stomach, a glimmer of fear and hope was starting to grow.

He took a step back, wondering what he should do next, before realizing that Dorothy was still waiting. Turning, he hurried back to his bedroom and picked up the receiver, before pausing for a moment. He knew he had to say something, but he didn't know what, not yet. All he could think about was the fact that suddenly the whole world seemed to be on the verge of a massive change.

"She's not home," he stammered, not wanting to cause a panic. "I'll tell her you called, though."

"Please do so," Dorothy replied. "Tell her I'm home all day, whenever she wants to call me back."

"I'll do that," he said, trying to sound polite. "Bye."

"And -"

"Bye."

Putting the phone down, he turned and looked toward the door. The house was still silent, but he was convinced that at any moment he'd hear her waking up. The thought that she was sick, or maybe even dead, was just too immense to contemplate, it simply wasn't how the universe worked. His grandmother was tough and strong, everyone knew that, she was the kind of leathery old battleaxe who'd live to a hundred or beyond. There was no way she could just drop dead in her early seventies. Still, as each second ticked past, he began to realize that the impossible was becoming more and more possible.

He also realized that he *wanted* her to be dead. He knew that made him a bad person, but he figured he could live with the guilt if it meant no more punishment, no more lectures and screaming. There was a part of him that thought he should rush back through and try to help her, that maybe she could be saved. At the same time, that thought – that she could be saved – horrified him.

So he stayed right where he was, listening to the silence.

Finally, after a few minutes, he realized he had to go and check. Heading back out to the landing, he made his way cautiously to her door and saw that she was still on the floor, still in exactly the same position as before.

He waited.

Watching.

Hoping.

"Gran?"

Stepping closer again, he got down onto his knees and then nudged her shoulder again. There was still no response, and he realized he couldn't see or hear any sign that she was breathing.

"Gran, can you hear me?"

He reached toward her neck to check for a pulse, but he pulled back as soon as he realized that her skin was cold to the touch. Instead, he placed two fingers against her frail wrist, waiting to feel a heartbeat, but there was nothing. Even though her skin felt ever-so-slightly rubbery, he moved his fingers a couple of times, convinced that at any moment he'd find that he was wrong and that she was perfectly okay. After a moment, he put a finger against her nose, not quite touching, but there was no hint of breath.

"Gran," he said firmly, "can you hear me?"

He nudged her shoulder again, a little harder this time, causing her body to shift slightly.

"Gran!"

Still trying not to panic, he realized he could feel his own heart racing. He had no idea what he was supposed to do next, but he didn't want to call an ambulance, not yet. His grandmother always hated having strangers in the house, and he knew she'd be mad at him if he let anyone inside unless their presence was strictly necessary. Besides, if he called them, they might be able to save her, and he didn't want that, not unless... Suddenly, he realized it might be a test, that she suspected he wouldn't do his best to help her. He froze, wondering what to do, before deciding that the whole situation was too good to be true.

There was no way she could be dead.

"I'm going to get you onto the bed," he told her, stepping to one side and then reaching down. He slipped his hands under her armpits and hauled her up, trying to be as delicate as possible as he dragged her toward and then up onto the bed, trying to ignore the growing realization that her arms and legs seemed a little stiff. He climbed up himself and pulled her body to the far end of the bed, before finally setting her down. Turning to check that her feet were on properly, he saw that she was only wearing one sock. This fact caused him to freeze for a moment, before he spotted a dark patch on the carpet where she'd been sitting. He took a few steps over to the wall before realizing he could smell old, stale urine.

He paused, before finally turning and seeing that his grandmother's eye and mouth had fallen open while he'd been moving her. Her eyes were staring straight up at the ceiling, while her mouth was sealed with a thin, milky white membrane, as if it had been closed for many hours.

"Thank you," he whispered, closing his eyes and feeling an immense sense of relief start to wash through his mind. "Thank you, thank you, thank you..."

CHAPTER FIVE

Today

"I'LL JUST BE A COUPLE MORE DAYS," he told Sarah over the phone as he made his way along the street. "I'll be back on Thursday, maybe Friday."

Stopping at the corner, he looked along Everley Street and saw the house waiting for him. He felt a sudden twitch in his gut, as if his belly was on the verge of flipping over entirely, but he knew it was too late to turn back now. He'd even left his car parked a few blocks back, so he could walk the rest of the way and recreate his old route home. For a man who never really got nostalgic about people, he certainly enjoyed being reunited with old streets and buildings from his youth.

"So are you still not going to tell me where

you are?" Sarah asked, as the children could be heard playing in the background.

"Just taking care of some business."

"What kind of business?"

"Nothing important."

"You're being mysterious," she continued. "What's wrong?"

"Nothing's wrong. I just..." He paused, before realizing that he was once again delaying things. "You'll see when I get back. It's a surprise. Trust me, you'll be very happy. If I told you now, it'd ruin the surprise. You're always complaining that I'm not very romantic these days, aren't you? Well, I'm doing something romantic for you right now, it'll just take a little while to pay off. Come on, get off my back on this one."

"Well you'd better be home when you say you will," she told him. "Romance is fine, but helping to look after the kids is better."

"I bet they've barely even noticed I'm gone."

"Sure they have," she replied. "Katie noticed the door to your writing room was open this morning. She was worried you'd been taken sick. She and Scott wanted to know where you'd gone, so I told them you were at an out-of-town book signing." She paused. "As long as you're not screwing some hot fan, I guess I can live with your absence for now."

"Come on," he replied, "you know me."

"I do. And I'm quite sure you're just moping around somewhere all by yourself. Have fun with that, honey."

Once the call was over, he stayed on the corner for a moment, still watching the house from a distance. He figured he'd have to come up with a surprise for Sarah, but he told himself he had plenty of time to worry about that later. Slipping the phone into his pocket, he made his way along the street, keeping his eyes fixed on the house and, in particular, on the upstairs window above the garage door. It had been twenty years since he'd last been in the house, but those twenty years suddenly felt as if they'd fallen away. He remembered the day he'd left, and he remembered how he'd sworn to never return, yet over the years he'd come to realize that he *had* to return.

He had to find out if the ghost had been real.

The house hadn't changed much, at least not from the outside. Tall and narrow, slightly over-built with a large wooden gable and bay windows, the place slightly out of skew with the line of the street, as if it had been dropped into position. The front garden was neat and tamed now, not wild like he'd left it, but all in all it was still by far the most imposing house on the street, and he felt he wasn't biased when he noted that all the other houses seemed more timid, as if they were shrugging back slightly. He'd dreamed of the house many times over the years, and now he saw that his dreams had been accurate. No detail had changed, and the whole place had stuck fast in his memory.

Taking the key from his pocket, he realized that yet again he was delaying things. Determined to get on with the task at hand, he made his way across the street and then swung the garden gate open, the same way he'd done years ago on his way back from school. Every footstep felt heavy, as if he was making his way back into the past, and by the time he got to the front door he was starting to remember the way his grandmother's cooking would always send smells wafting out to meet him. It had never occurred to him until that moment that he might have a visceral physical reaction to this return journey, but now he could feel his body shifting into a different gear. There was a part of him that wanted to turn and run, but at the same time he knew he could never do that. He owed it to himself to at least take a look around, and to at least spend one final night inside.

He slipped the key into the lock, and a moment later he swung the door open.

The house smelled different.

After stepping into the hallway, he pushed the door shut and then stood for a moment, looking around. As he'd expected, the new owners had made some major changes, but the basic layout of the place was still the same. He looked over at the stairs and immediately remembered the morning, twenty years ago, when he'd sat there and picked up the phone to call for an ambulance. He wanted to reach out and tell that scared teenager that everything would be okay, and he swallowed hard as he made his way to the kitchen. Stopping again, he was hit by more memories: he remembered his grandmother cooking at the old stove, and he remembered when he used to sit at the breakfast bar in the corner and eat his breakfast before school. The room had changed beyond recognition now, of course, and the wall through to the old garage had been partially knocked down and replaced by an archway. Still, it was the same space, the same house.

The door to the basement was still over by the far wall.

Turning, he headed to the front room. More memories came flooding back as he walked past the spot where his grandmother's TV armchair had once stood, and he stopped at the window and looked out at the back garden. His grandmother had been a keen gardener and had cultivated a strong lineage of fuchsia plants, which had won several prizes at local shows. The garden had been completely changed in the intervening years, however, and the new owners had covered the lawn with paving stones, turning it into a kind of patio that seemed a little cramped in such a small space. He was glad that the place wasn't the same as it had been in the old days, and that it had been lived in, although he was surprised by just how much had been altered. He had to keep reminding himself that it was the same building in which he'd lived all those years ago.

"Welcome home," he muttered to himself, before glancing at the ceiling and realizing that he still had to go and look at the upstairs rooms. If there was still a ghost in the house on Everley Street, that was where she'd be.

CHAPTER SIX

Twenty years ago

"SHE WAS JUST ON THE FLOOR," he said blankly, sitting at the foot of the stairs as he spoke to his father on the phone. It was late now, almost midnight, but the timezone difference meant that he'd had to wait until early evening before calling, and even then he'd had to try several times and leave a message with his father's assistant before finally getting a callback. "They said it was probably an aneurysm, but they're going to let me know for sure."

"Jesus," his father replied, sounding tired. "At least aneurysms are fairly quick. What kind of aneurysm was it? Cerebral? Aortic?"

"I don't know."

"Was it thoracic? They must have have a few ideas."

"They just said it was an aneurysm."

"But if -"

"It's all been kind of a blur," he added, hoping to shut off the flow of incessant questions. Reaching back, he scratched one of the cigarette burns on his shoulder. "They said she might have felt a little weak just before it happened. They didn't know why she'd sat down on the floor, but they thought maybe she'd tried to get out of bed during the night and her legs had given way. Even so, they said she probably didn't suffer. She probably just slipped away, like she was going to sleep." He paused. "Which I guess is good."

In his mind's eye, he saw her dead face again, with her eyes staring up at the ceiling. It was an image that had been constantly filling his thoughts all day, interrupting everything else, and he'd spent most of his time running through the precise series of events in order, obsessively trying to remember every moment of the discovery. He figured maybe he was in shock, although he didn't really know what to do about that fact. Ride it out, maybe, and just wait for it to pass.

"So she might have been calling out to you for help?" his father asked.

At this, John paused. "I didn't hear anything," he said cautiously, glancing up at the dark landing at the top of the stairs. He waited, half expecting to hear some sign of movement. "I slept the whole night through. I only woke up so early because someone phoned for her."

"And you're there now?"

"In the house?" He swallowed hard. "Yeah."

"Are you okay?"

He paused. The question was unexpected, and he couldn't remember the last time his father had asked him something so personal. "I -"

"It's good that you're not freaking out," his father added, cutting him off. "It must have been a shock for you to find her like that, but what's done is done. Everything's going to be okay."

"I know," John whispered.

"And there's really nothing to worry about," his father continued. "Try to get an early night, sleep's always the best medicine in a situation like this. You need to give your brain time to rest and heal, let your subconscious mind do its stuff and absorb everything. I won't keep you talking for too long."

"I don't mind."

"It's late for you. And I have meetings."

"But..." He paused. "She'd wet herself," he added finally.

"She'd what?"

"She'd wet herself. There was a stain on the carpet. I need to go and clean it."

"Yeah, people do piss themselves when they die," his father muttered. "You're lucky it was just that. Sometimes the bowels loosen too and you end up with the old brown stuff everywhere."

John flinched at the directness. Still, he wanted to talk about the discovery of the body some more, in as much detail as possible. Somehow, it made him feel better.

"She wasn't a bad woman," his father continued, "even though we had our disagreements over the years. I don't think she ever thought I was really good enough for her precious daughter, but I guess that's a story for another day. I guess she blamed me for your mother's..." He paused. "Well, you know what I mean. Listen, buddy, you must let me know when you've arranged the funeral and I'll book a flight. I won't be able to stay for too long, just a night or two, but I'll definitely do my best to come. I know it's probably a lot for you to handle on our own, but look online if you're stuck with anything. There are loads of sites that'll tell you exactly what you have to do. Of course, we'll have to talk about the house, too. When I bought it for the pair of you to live in, I never really had a long-term plan. This definitely puts a spanner in the works, but it might be an opportunity too."

"When I found her," John replied, "and when I moved her, her mouth opened and -"

"I should let you go," his father said,

interrupting him.

"Her mouth opened -"

"Give me a call tomorrow if you like. I'm busy most of the day, but I'll be free between about half five and quarter to six. I'm not sure what time that is where you are, you'll need to work it out. What's the difference? Six, seven hours? But chin up, kid, yeah? It's probably all for the best in the long-run, really. I know that sounds harsh, but I think a change could really help to spur you on. Now go and get a good night's sleep. Hey, did your grandmother still keep a bottle of port or sherry on the sideboard?"

"I think so."

"Take a glass or two. I know you don't like drinking alcohol, but it'll settle you down."

"Maybe."

"Not maybe. Definitely."

"Sure."

"And try to look at this as a good thing," his father added. "Your grandmother was fine in her own way, and it's always sad when someone dies, but she could also be... I mean, you know she wasn't all there in the head, don't you? Some of the things your mother used to tell me, well, they were pretty shocking. Your grandmother was a strange old bird, and she was making you strange too, so looking on the bright side, I can't deny that I'm glad you'll be getting out from under her shadow. One day, you'll look back on this as the first day of the rest of your life."

***

A few minutes later, once the call was over, John crouched next to the stain on the carpet and began to slowly pour out some bleach. He knew there were better ways to clean the place, but he just wanted to nuke the whole thing and get rid of the urine smell, maybe even rip up the carpet in a day or two. Adding way more bleach than he knew was reasonable, he finally got to his feet and took a step back, before looking over at the bed.

For a moment, all he could think about was the way his grandmother's eyes and mouth had fallen open when he'd moved her. That was when he'd known, really known for certain, that she was gone. The worst part was, there had been just a hint of relief in his chest. He knew he was a bad person for thinking such things, but life in his grandmother's house had been difficult for many years and he'd been trying to work out how he could get away. He'd even tried taking a Saturday job at the local supermarket, but his social skills were non-existent and he'd lasted a little less than three shifts. His grandmother had always found ways to make him stay at home, to make him feel as if leaving was impossible, and over time he'd come to believe her, to accept that his life was going to be mostly lived in that cramped house. Now, suddenly, she was gone. The worst part, the part that really made him feel guilty, was that he hadn't even cried yet.

"You're no use out there," he remembered her telling him once. "You're not a people person."

"I could try," he'd replied.

"There's no point putting yourself through it. Just accept who you are."

As hard as he tried, he couldn't shake the sense of freedom. Freedom to think about the future, not just vague ideas but actual plans, things he could get out there and do, and freedom make mistakes without getting burned. He even had the freedom now to sleep in his own bed without having to let her climb in and sleep next to him, sometimes with her arm around his shoulder. He'd never said as much to her, but he'd always hated that and he knew it wasn't normal for a seventeen-year-old boy to live that way, but at the same time he'd felt powerless to stop her.

And now she was gone.

Really, truly, finally gone.

He knew it was probably sad, but he didn't *feel* sad. He hoped she hadn't suffered, that she hadn't known what was happening and that she hadn't been calling out to him while he slept, begging for help. Still, it was too late to worry too much. It was over.

"Goodbye," he whispered, although he immediately felt a little silly for saying anything.

With the room filling up with the smell of bleach, he made his way to the window and opened it as far as he could, before heading out of the room and pulling the door shut. He took a step back and took a deep breath of cleaner air, and he told himself that there was really no reason to go into that room again. He could just leave the door shut and forget that there was a room in there at all, and he could spend his time planning what he was going to do next. His grandmother's death had been so sudden and unexpected, he hadn't had time so far to come up with anything more than a few vague notions.

More than anything, he wanted to be a writer, just like his mother had wanted to be, but he had no idea where to start.

Heading downstairs, he found the bottles of port his grandmother had left in the cabinet and he quickly poured them away. Then, filled with an urge to keep tidying even though it was well past midnight, he took the vacuum cleaner from the closet and began to clean the house. He'd always been good at his chores, but this time he couldn't hold back and he made sure to vacuum every inch of every carpet in all the downstairs rooms, preferring the loud roar of the machine to the calm, quiet stillness of the house. Once he'd finished, he put the vacuum cleaner away and decided to started bagging up some of his grandmother's possessions, so he grabbed some black sacks and started going through things in the front room. Feeling uncomfortable with the silence, he switched the TV on and turned the volume up, not even bothering to change the channel as he got back to work. Some late-night sitcom babbled along in the background, followed by another and then another, and by the time he'd filled up six sacks with his grandmother's things, he saw to his surprise that it was already 4am.

Too late, he figured, to go to bed now.

Might as well just work through the night.

So that's what he did, finding job after job until the sun came up. He emptied his grandmother's food from the fridge, and then he cleaned out the pantry cupboards, and then he started going through the laundry, getting rid of all her clothes. Soon he had eight sacks filled, then twelve, then he got to sixteen and ran out of sacks entirely. Starting to use plastic bags from the supermarket instead, he continued to clean, with the TV still running all the while in the background so that he wouldn't have to worry about the silence all around. He stayed downstairs the whole time, until finally the sun began to rise higher in the morning sky and cast a warm orange glow through the kitchen window, and he realized he'd managed to make it through the night.

Exhausted, he headed to the front room and turned the TV off. Silence fell, and he stood for a moment, listening to the house, waiting for any hint of movement.

There was nothing.

He was truly alone.

Heading upstairs, he made his way to the bathroom and went to the toilet, before washing his face. He felt strangely free, as if the long night's work had helped him to mark a transition. Leaning closer to the mirror, he saw his own dry eyes staring back at him, and he realized that he couldn't manufacture a sense of loss where no such thing existed. Although he felt bad for his grandmother, he was also glad that he never had to feel her arm around him again while he tried to sleep, and he never had to listen to her complain that he wasn't doing enough to take his mother's place. It was his mother's death, more than anything, that had been held over his head and used to keep him under control.

Turning, he headed out of the bathroom, but after a moment he stopped suddenly. A flash of fear rippled through his chest as he saw that the door to his grandmother's bedroom, which he remembered closing several hours earlier, was now wide open.

CHAPTER SEVEN

Today

THE DOOR TO HER OLD BEDROOM WAS OPEN, but he figured it had just been left that way by the family who'd moved out a few days earlier. After all, the other doors were open too, and he told himself that the days were long gone when he'd allow his fears to build.

Stepping into the room, he couldn't help but smile as he saw that bright, patterned wallpaper had been put up, featuring pictures of animals and flowers. Somewhere over the past twenty years, the room had been turned into a nursery, and when he looked down at the spot where he'd found his grandmother's body, he realized that there were four soft indentations in the new carpet, tell-tale signs that a crib had only recently been taken out. He headed over to the window and slid it open, letting some air in, before turning to look back around at the room.

He waited.

Silence.

"Gran?" he said out loud. He knew he was being foolish, but he couldn't help himself, not now he felt so certain that he was alone. For the past twenty years, he'd worried that she was still in the house, still waiting for him, but now the idea seemed preposterous. In fact, he was starting to think that he'd spent two decades building himself up to an event that was now not going to deliver a damn thing. He'd been plotting to buy the house, telling himself that he could finally work out whether his grandmother's spirit lingered, and it had never occurred to him that he'd one day get back and find that it really *was* just a house.

Just some walls and floors and ceilings, and empty space in-between.

No ghost.

"Gran?" he said again, allowing himself a faint smile. He made his way back to the door and then turned to look down at the spot where he'd found her. "Gran, are you here?"

No answer.

"Hello?" he called out. "Anyone? If you're around, give me a sign. Rattle a door, or bump against the wall."

He waited.

Nothing.

"I guess not," he muttered, feeling a little foolish. Still, he remembered what it had been like twenty years ago, when he'd been left alone in the house and he'd started to hear sounds. Scratches on the walls, whispers around the corners... He'd long known that there was a chance he'd simply been an impressionable kid, but he'd told himself he couldn't have imagined everything that had happened. Now, however, in the cold light of day he felt increasingly certain that the whole thing *had* been entirely in his head. His grandmother had died, and that had been the end of it. The only thing she'd left behind, besides her body, had been the stain on the carpet, and now even that was gone.

Still, the trip wouldn't be a total waste. There was one other thing he still had to do while he was in town.

***

"I'm sorry I didn't come back sooner," he whispered, looking down at his mother's grave. "I mean, I always knew I'd come and see you again eventually, but..."

He paused, feeling slightly foolish for saying the words out loud, before crouching down and setting a bunch of yellow roses on the grass, just ahead of the gravestone. His mother had always loved yellow roses, or at least that was what he'd been told by his father. He didn't remember enough to be certain.

"Life just got in the way," he continued. "Can you believe that? I never used to have much of a life at all. Just sitting around, watching TV and writing and reading, and occasionally going to the shops with Gran. It's not like school was exactly fun, either, but... Well, I guess I shouldn't complain."

He began to rearrange the roses, before realizing that they were fine as they were.

"Do you remember how you used to write stories and then read then to me?" he asked. "I know you always wanted to be a writer, but... That's what I do now, can you believe it? You're the one who made me want to tell stories, and now I tell the kind of stories that other people like turning into big, blockbuster movies. You'd probably hate them." He paused, remembering the days when, as a child, he used to sit on his mother's while she read the latest story she'd come up with. "I wish I still had some of your stuff," he told her. "Just one of your stories would be enough, but... Then again, I don't even have a photo of you. I remember what you looked like, that's not a problem, but a photo would be good. Still, it's my fault, isn't it? I should have taken care of the few photos I once had."

Reaching down, he placed a hand against the grass.

"I don't know when I'll get another chance to come," he told her. "I figure I'll head off tomorrow, back to London. That's where I live now, I'm married to a woman named Sarah. We have two children, Katie and Scott, and we live a pretty good life. Things were tough for a while back there, but I really turned it around. More by luck than judgment, but I sort of bounced off various possibilities until I reached a decent place."

He paused, before checking over his shoulder to make sure that no-one was around to see him talking to himself. He knew he was being a little weird, but he didn't care.

"I don't blame you anymore," he continued, looking back down at the grave. "For leaving me alone with her, I mean. I know there was nothing else you could have done, everything just became too much for you and it's not like Dad was any help. I just wish..."

His voice trailed off for a moment as he remembered that moment, years ago, when he'd heard his mother's agonized screams. His grandmother had been trying to help her, but even as a child he'd understood that it was too late. No-one could be in so much pain and survive, and sure enough the screams had stopped long before the ambulance showed up. Later, he'd overheard snatches of conversation about what had really happened, and his grandmother had been brutally honest.

"You know bleach?" she'd said, sitting on the edge of his bed. "The stuff we use to clean? Well, your mother drank some, and it burned her up from the inside out."

He remembered seeing the body being carried out of the old house, and then he remembered his grandmother packing his things and hurrying him out the door, heading to her place on Everley Street.

"Gran was the only one who'd take me in after you were gone," he continued, "so it was natural that I stayed with her. I guess I was angry for a while, but..." He paused again. "I know she was difficult when you were alive, but your death really made her worse. She got so bitter and angry, it was really hard living with her. I'd like to think that even if she hadn't died, I'd have left eventually, but the truth is, I was completely dependent. I'd probably still be there now, living under her thumb and..."

He paused, worrying that he was sounding a little pathetic. Reaching into his pocket, he took out his phone and brought up a photo of Sarah and the children. He knew it was crazy to get so sentimental, and a little mawkish too, but he couldn't help himself. Turning the phone toward the gravestone, he allowed himself a faint smile.

"Mum, meet Sarah, Scott and Katie. You guys, meet my mother."

He took a deep breath.

"I should get back to them. It's crazy of me to hang around this place, reliving everything that happened twenty years ago. I should be focusing on my life as it is now, not the way it used to be." He took a look at the photo of his family, before slipping the phone away. "I'm going to stop feeling so sorry for myself. I have a great life, really, and it's been mostly due to sheer fluke, but hell, I can't do anything about that. Bad things have happened, but they're outweighed by the good. I see that now. I can't let myself get dragged back into this place. I have to leave the house behind. She's not there, and even if she was..."

Getting to his feet, he began to button his coat as he felt a chill wind blowing across the cemetery.

"Alright," he muttered, "one more afternoon and one more night in that house and then I'm out of here for good."

CHAPTER EIGHT

Twenty years ago

"JOHN!"

Opening his eyes suddenly, he stared up at the dark ceiling. It was his second night alone in the house and he'd finally managed to get some sleep, mainly due to exhaustion from his previous night's cleaning frenzy. He'd been dreaming, he knew that much, although he couldn't remember the details. A voice had woken him, however, and with a slow, creeping sense of dread he realized that he knew exactly whose voice it had been.

Turning, he looked toward the bedroom door, half expecting to see a figure out on the dark landing.

There was no-one.

He waited, listening to the silence of the house, trying to convince himself that the voice had simply been a part of his dream, but he'd heard it just as he was on the cusp of waking up, which meant he couldn't be sure whether it had come from the dream or from the real world. He told himself that it was natural for him to be jumpy, and that there was no-one else in the house and that his grandmother's soul, if she'd even had one to begin with, was long gone along with her body. Still, he could tell that something felt wrong, even if he couldn't quite put his finger on the source of the problem, and with each passing second he expected to hear her voice again, calling out to him.

Somehow, deep in his bones, he felt that he wasn't alone.

"Please don't," he whispered. "Please, please don't come back."

Deep down, he felt certain that she'd called out to him two nights ago, on the night when she'd died. He was sure she must have begged for him to wake up, but he figured he must have just slept through it all. He tried to imagine himself sleeping soundly, not hearing the faint, plaintive cries from the other bedroom.

And now she was gone.

Letting his head settle back on the pillow, he stared at the window, waiting for tiredness to return. Ghosts didn't exist, he knew that. After all, his mother had died several years earlier and he felt certain that if people could come back and contact the living, she'd have appeared a long time ago. He told himself that he was simply struggling to deal with the silence of the house, and that it was natural for him to start having dark dreams, but he was also sure that he could withstand any hint of paranoia. His grandmother had told him he was weak, but he was starting to feel strong.

"There's no such thing as ghosts," he heard his own voice saying at the back of his mind, like a mantra. "There's no such thing as ghosts. She's gone."

He waited, but even though he hadn't heard her voice again, he was certain that something felt wrong. The silence of the house was starting to build again, to sound the way it had sounded on the morning when he found her body. He turned to look at the door again, and although he knew he was probably imagining it all, he was suddenly filled with the overwhelming sense that if he just went out and walked to her bedroom door, he'd see her again, down there on the floor. The idea was impossible to entertain, of course, but he could still feel it tugging at the edge of his mind, and finally he realized that he'd never be able to get to sleep if he didn't at least go and check.

Slowly, he got out of bed and made his way to the door.

"You only have to do this once," he told himself. "Go and look, prove that she's not there, and then you'll know forever. That's how it works."

He paused, trying to believe his own advice.

"John."

He froze. He'd heard the voice again, except it took only a fraction of a second for him to have doubts. *Had* he heard it, or had it just been a brief surge in the silence? Reaching out, he switched on the landing light and saw that there was no sign of anyone near the top of the stairs. His mind was racing, thinking back to the voice and trying desperately to work out whether it had been real or not. He told himself that it couldn't be, that it was far more likely that he was on the verge of cracking up, but more than ever now he knew that he had to go and look in her bedroom.

"John," the voice had whispered.

Slowly, with fear tightening in his chest, he began to make his way along the landing until he reached her door. It was shut, of course, just the way he'd left it when he went to bed.

He took a deep breath.

"Hello?" he called out, although he instantly regretted saying anything, in case somehow the mere words might summon his grandmother's spirit when otherwise she'd stay away.

He reached out for the handle, but still he hesitated. He tried to imagine what it would be like to open the door and see her dead face staring back at him from the darkness.

"If she's there," he told himself, "you'll know you can never escape her. If she's not there, you'll know she's gone forever. Either way, at least you'll know for certain and -"

Stopping suddenly, he realized that he'd started talking to himself. Wasn't that one of the signs of madness? Then again, it was the only way to organize his thoughts. Taking another deep breath, he took hold of the handle and pushed the door open, letting it swing slowly until it bumped against the wall.

The room was dark, too dark to see anything.

"Hello?" he whispered.

Silence.

"John," he imagined her saying, and after a moment he realized that the silence in the room was hissing slightly, as if her voice might emerge at any moment. At the same time, the darkness seemed to be shifting, and it wasn't hard to picture her dead face slowly getting closer, with her mouth still wide open and covered with the white gum of death. He stood his ground, imagining her looming toward him, imagining her wild, unblinking eyes fixed on him.

"Why didn't you wake up?" he imagined her asking. "I was calling out for you, begging for help.

Why did you stay asleep?"

Now he imagined her face right against his, with her mouth still gummed. And then, slowly, he felt her thin, bony fingers starting to rest on his shoulders, and suddenly he couldn't tell whether they were really there or not.

Reaching out, he flicked the switch on the wall. As soon as the light was on, he looked around the bare room and saw to his relief that there was no sign of anyone. It had all been in his head. He made his way over to the bed and forced himself to stay in the room for a moment, determined not to run like a coward. In the back of his mind, he felt that this was the best way to get rid of any crazy ideas at the root, to prove to himself beyond a shadow of a doubt that ghosts didn't exist and that his grandmother wasn't haunting the place. He knew the if that seed was allowed to grow in his mind, it could overwhelm him, so he went back to the wall and flicked the light off again, before waiting in the dark with his back to both the bed and the spot where he'd found his grandmother's body. He was tempting her, waiting for her to take her chance. Finally, he got down onto his knees, still with his back to the darkened room, still daring her to make her presence known.

"Come on," he whispered. "If you're here, do something."

He waited.

After a moment, he could almost feel a cold hand slithering onto his shoulder and starting to pull him back. He told himself it wasn't there, that his imagination was filling in the gaps, and deep down he knew that was true; at the same time, he couldn't help himself and he continued to imagine her edging closer with dark, dead eyes.

And then he imagined her voice, too.

"You let me die," she whispered. "You could have helped me, but you wanted me dead."

"No," he replied, "I just... It was too late, you were already gone."

"Liar. Dirty, filthy little liar."

He shook his head.

"I'm still here, you know," she continued. "The other you can't hide everything forever. I'm not going to let you go so easily."

He was breathing faster now, while still trying to stay calm as he felt her wrapping her arms around him from behind, pulling him tight into a dead embrace and breathing against the back of his neck, and then he felt several burning pains all over his back, as if she was punishing him. Still, he knew none of it was really happening, and finally he let the image drift away, leaving him still kneeling on the floor in the darkened room. Turning finally, he looked over his shoulder and saw to his relief that there was still no sign of her.

He'd imagined it all.

Which meant, he told himself, that the house definitely wasn't haunted. Still, he couldn't help worrying, so he went to the bathroom and pulled his t-shirt up, before turning to examine his back in the mirror.

Along with the old scars, there were half a dozen fresh burn marks, still blistering into his flesh.

CHAPTER NINE

Today

HE COULD ALREADY HEAR voices from the other side of the door.

"They should totally stop and wait for the books to catch up," an excited girl was saying. "They can't diverge much further from what Martin writes or it won't be an adaptation anymore, will it? It'll be, like, an alternate history, and who wants that? Why don't they stop making it for a few years?"

"But Martin's basically telling them what to write anyway!"

"I don't care, you can't adapt a book that hasn't been written yet!"

Sighing, John considered *not* knocking.

Having always avoided interviews, press events and even book launches except for the bare minimum, he had no idea why he'd suddenly decided to turn up to some dumb little book club run by a bunch of kids, especially since it sounded as if they were having the kind of mind-numbingly unnecessary discussion he could already hear before he'd even walked through the door. After a moment, however, he realized that he *did* know why he'd shown up, even if he didn't want to admit it. He felt that, by returning to his childhood home and facing the (lack of) demons, he'd passed over a threshold and now he wanted to mark that fact by becoming more open, more real. He wanted to surprise himself.

So he knocked on the door, felt a shiver of apprehension, and waited.

"I don't know," a guy's voice could be heard saying. "Everyone's here. Who ordered pizza?"

"Not me," the girl's voice replied, "but I won't say no."

A moment later, the door swung open, bringing John face to face with a thin, gangly teenager wearing an old *Masters of the Universe* t-shirt.

"Oh my God!" Hannah said, hurrying to the doorway with barely concealed glee. "John Myers! You came!"

***

"Uh, no," John replied with a frown and a smile, "I honestly never thought of it like that. Lucardo wasn't intended as an allegory for Christ, not at all."

"Okay," said Hannah, "sorry, I was wrong. I get carried away sometimes, my teachers at school always told me I had a tendency to let my imagination go way overboard."

"Well, no," he continued, "you weren't *wrong* necessarily, it's just not something I intended when I was writing *The Revenge of Lucardo Hitch*, but that doesn't mean it's not a valid reading of the text. In fact, now you mention it, there are definitely points where an allegorical interpretation would..." He paused for a moment, realizing that he was starting to drone on and on like his old English Lit professor. He looked over at a bunch of Miyazaki and Jacques Tati posters on the wall, feeling momentarily as if he was far too old to be hanging out with a bunch of kids, before finally turning back to them. He couldn't deny that their admiration made him feel good. "You know what? You guys seem to know my books better than I do. I barely even remember the plot of *Lucardo Hitch*, it's been a decade since it came out."

"You barely remember one of your own novels?" Gary asked.

"I tend to move on once they're done," he explained. "I don't dwell on things. Well, not when it comes to my work, anyway."

"I've read all your books," Hannah told him, staring at him with wide-eyed enthusiasm. It was the kind of stare he'd never received before, not even from his own wife, and he couldn't deny that it was flattering. "Some of them twice."

"Even the bad ones?" he asked with a faint smile.

"Oh, yes," she replied earnestly. "Even the bad ones."

"There are a lot of books out there," he said cautiously. "Personally I only re-read the ones that are really important to me."

"Me too," she replied.

"This is so amazing," Hannah continued, turning to the couple of other guys who'd turned up for the book club. "I told you he'd come. I know you thought I was making it all up, but I knew deep down that he'd show."

"What about ghosts?" asked Louis, one of the other members of the group. "One thing I never really got from reading your books, and from reading interviews with you, is your real-life view on ghosts. Do you think they actually exist?"

"Tough question," John replied, feeling as if he wasn't quite ready to give a straight answer. "What about you guys? Do *you* think ghosts exist?"

"Totally," Louis said, and the others nodded in agreement.

John paused, well aware that they were now waiting for him to tell them what he thought. "Sometimes I believe," he said finally, "and sometimes I don't. My rational mind says that no, they can't exist, that we'd have evidence if they were real. My rational mind says that with all the camera-phones around these days, and all the equipment that even amateur ghost-hunters can buy online, the lack of documented proof is deafening. At the same time, in the right situation, I start to wonder. I get that same nagging feeling, tugging at me, telling me that maybe there's something else in the cosmos, something behind the things I know about. I think that's a pretty universal human trait." Another pause. "Which I guess means that I don't believe, not really. I just like scaring myself late at night. Sorry, is that a disappointing answer?"

"Not at all," Hannah told him. "It's just so cool that you can write about them even though you have doubts. You make ghosts seem so real."

He smiled, even though he knew he was in danger of liking her compliments a little too much. Still, he figured it was all harmless enough.

"But it's kind of weird," Louis pointed out, "I mean... You've made your career out of writing about something you think is a crock of... Well, you know what I mean."

"So you're saying I'm a professional liar?"

"No, but... It just seems weird that you'd

spend so much time writing about ghosts if you don't think they could possibly exist."

"But people *think* they exist," he replied. "That phenomenon itself, the belief, is kind of interesting, don't you think? I want to know why people believe in ghosts, why they think they see them, why they create those fantasies. A good lie can be as fascinating as the truth."

"But it's almost like you're... I don't know, making fun of people who believe."

"I'm definitely not making fun of anyone," John continued, starting to feel a little as if he was under attack. "If someone wants to see a ghost, the mind can be a powerful thing and I absolutely understand why they could truly believe it's happening. That doesn't make the person dumb or sick, it just means they lean in one particular direction."

"So you think people only see ghosts if they want to?"

"On a subconscious level, maybe."

"So you've never seen one?" Hannah asked, butting in. "You've never even suspected there's one around?"

"I..." He paused, aware that she seemed a little more pointed with her questions, as if she was lightly interrogating him. The others in the room seemed more random, but he couldn't shake the feeling that Hannah had an agenda. His natural paranoia, perhaps, was starting to show.

"Not even once?" she continued, clearly keen for him to answer. "Not even a hint?"

"I've had my moments," he replied, choosing his words with care. "There have been times when I've been convinced that a ghost would appear, but..." He paused, thinking back to the old days in his grandmother's house. "I guess I just have a limit to how much I can believe in a fantasy. I truly believe that if ghosts were real, I'd have seen one properly by now."

"Because you've been in a situation where a ghost would definitely appear to you," she asked, "if it had the chance?"

"Something like that."

"Isn't that kind of patronizing?" Louis asked. "It's like you're saying you're too smart to fool yourself, but other people can do it just fine."

"I didn't say that -"

"Leave him be!" Hannah said, nudging Louis. "Jeez, you're being kinda rude! The guy's entitled to his opinions."

"I just want to know what he thinks," Louis replied defensively.

"I think the human mind is a complex thing," John said, hoping to keep them from fighting. He enjoyed the way Hannah seemed to be on his side, and even if he didn't want to admit that he found her attractive, he also wanted to keep her attention. Not that he'd ever cheat on his wife, but still, he figured that talking to a pretty girl wasn't illegal. "I was once in a situation," he said cautiously, "where I truly believed that someone I knew was going to come back and appear to me as a ghost. It wasn't too far from here, actually. I was certain, absolutely convinced without a shadow of doubt, that she'd appear to me. In fact, she'd actually told me, specifically, that if she died, she'd come back and haunt me."

"What kind of person says that?" Gary asked.

"A messed-up, manipulative person, in this instance," John continued with a faint smile. He felt a little uncomfortable being so open, but at the same time, he couldn't help himself. "So I was more than certain, given her nature and given the circumstances, that she'd show up. And I was more than vulnerable, I was a sitting duck, I even dared her. I goaded her, I told her to show herself. She had ample time to make her presence known in one way or another, but..." He paused.

"She didn't?" Hannah asked, with a hint of disappointment in her voice.

"She didn't. Nothing. I imagined her coming back, I built it up in my head, I was terrified at times and I even dreamed about it, but I realized later that it never actually happened. There were no spooky goings on at all. I mean, maybe a few bumps in the night, but nothing that couldn't be rationally explained. Trust me, though, if she could have come back and haunted me, she'd have done so." He paused again, feeling as if he was opening up for the first time, and wondering why he was telling these kids something he hadn't even told his wife or his so-called friends. "At the same time," he continued, "I carried the fear of her everywhere I went. For the past twenty years, I've slightly expected her to show up at any moment, so I guess you could say she was haunting me that way. Or rather, I was haunting myself. And then recently..."

He glanced at Hannah and saw that she was hooked on his every word.

"Recently," he added, addressing her and only her now, "I had the opportunity to face my fear once and for all. Just today, actually. And guess what? The house was empty, there was nothing there. Of course there wasn't, there never was, but that didn't stop me building it up over the years. Tonight I'll be sleeping in the place that I once thought she haunted, and by doing so I'll be permanently wiping away the last vestiges of doubt, getting rid of those little whispers at the corner of my mind. The prospect is both intimidating and freeing. I feel like a major part of my life is changing."

"So..." Gary paused, frowning, "you're going to spend tonight in a haunted house?"

"Can we come?" Hannah asked immediately.

"I have an electro-spectrometer," Gary said. "It needs a big battery, but I can fit it in my backpack."

"I've got infra-red goggles," Louis added. "And a camera."

"I don't need company," John replied, amused by their eagerness, "and it's not a haunted house. It's just a house. In fact, if anyone in that place is a ghost, it's me, still clinging to the past and letting it define me." He sighed. "But not after tonight. After tonight, I'm going to be a new man, because I'm going to do what we should all do when we get the opportunity. I'm going to face my fears." Pausing, he smiled, realizing that he'd gone a little too far into his personal beliefs than he'd intended. "And that, if you want one, is tonight's lesson. Jesus, I promised myself I wouldn't turn into some moralizing old fart, but here I am, offering you a bunch of Hallmark life lessons. You're very welcome."

"What if you can't write after that?" Louis asked.

John turned to him.

"What if all your inspiration goes? Like... What if you can only write because of who you used to be, and after tonight you won't be able to do it anymore?"

"Well..." John paused. "Then I guess I'll have to start writing in a different genre. Maybe -"

Before he could finish, he felt his phone vibrating, and he pulled it from his pocket just in time to see his wife's name flashing up on the screen. For a moment he considered not answering, so that he could keep talking to the others, particularly to Hannah, but finally he realized he needed to get back to reality. He was a married man with two children, and he needed to say goodnight to them before bedtime.

"My wife," he told them, feeling as if he was perhaps disappointing Hannah a little. And himself. Getting to his feet, he answered the call and headed through to the kitchen of the cramped flat, hoping to get some privacy. The room was pretty filthy, with old pizza boxes everywhere and wine bottles that had been turned into candle-sticks. "Hey," he said, unable to suppress a grimace as he saw piles of dirty plates and discarded food all over the place, "what's up?"

"Oh, it's late and I thought I'd check in and see if my husband is still alive," Sarah replied airily. "Seeing as you're being all mysterious lately n'all. How are things going, anyway? Do you want to finally tell me what you're doing?"

"Right now?" He paused with a faint, mischievous smile. "Right now, I'm at a meeting of a small sci-fi and horror book club, talking about my life and work with some fans. Discussing my personal beliefs, a little of my life story here and there, some jokes and observations. It's very relaxed."

"Ha ha," she said flatly. "And let me guess, you rode there on a unicorn, huh? Seriously? You, at some kind of social event? Pull the other one, John, it's got bells on. If you're going to lie, at least be plausible."

"I can be social."

"No, honey, you can't. I love you, you know that, but you really aren't a sociable best. Not voluntarily, anyway. You have many magnificent qualities, but that's not one of them."

"I can fake it, though."

"No, you can't."

"I faked it at that book launch the other night."

"Nope."

"I did!"

"Sorry, honey. Everyone could tell how much you hated it." She sighed. "Okay, have your little secret. I just wanted to say goodnight, and that the kids and I miss you, and that every second you're away is another favor that you owe me. The kids are officially on holiday now, and they seem to have more energy than ever. We're supposed to split parenting duties right down the middle, remember? Please don't make me nag."

"I'll be back tomorrow," he replied, as he spotted Gary in the doorway. "Hold on, Sarah. I think someone wants my attention."

"Mr. Myers," Gary said, "we were wondering -"

He stopped as John held his phone up, allowing his wife to hear.

"Go on," John said with a smile.

"Well... We were wondering if, before you go tonight, you could talk to us a little more about the inspiration for your writing, particularly in terms of the difference between supernatural horror and horror that's grounded in the way people are just totally cruel to each other. Torture and body horror, that kind of thing. It's like, you know, we're such big fans and this is such a rare opportunity, and talking to you has been so cool."

John moved the phone closer to his face. "That's fine, Gary," he said with a grin, imagining Sarah's reaction. "I'd be happy to do that. Tell Hannah and the others that I'll be through in just a moment to continue our fascinating discussion."

As Gary headed back to the main room, John put the phone to the side of his face.

There was nothing but silence on the other end.

"I have to go," he said after a moment, "the others are waiting for me. It's been a really interesting book club and I think everyone's learning a lot."

He waited for a reply, but he could almost hear Sarah's jaw hitting the ground on the other end.

"Honey?" he said. "Are you still there?"

"Okay," she said finally, with a hint of caution in her voice, "who are you, and what have you done with my husband?"

CHAPTER TEN

Twenty years ago

"HEY," ALISON SAID WITH A SMILE, as soon as John opened the door. She was wearing a cream sweater with a big ladybird on the front. "Long time, stranger."

Startled, he stared at her for a moment. He'd spent the morning tidying the house, lost in his own thoughts... or at least that was what he told himself. For a moment, he felt as if maybe there was something he'd forgotten, as if his mind had divided into two completely separate halves, but that sensation passed quickly enough. Instead, he focused on the surprise of seeing Alison standing in front of him. After all, she was one of his few friends, or at least she had been, back when he still *had* friends, back in his school days.

"Are you gonna invite me in?" she asked, raising a skeptical eyebrow, "or do I have to force my way through the door? Which, to be fair, wouldn't be so easy after my recent op." She looked down at his foot. "Are you limping?"

"Oh, it's nothing," he replied. "I just hurt my toe when..." Pausing, he realized he didn't remember how he'd hurt it. "It's nothing. Come in."

***

"Wow," she said a few minutes later, looking out the window and watching the fuchsia plants for a moment before turning back to him, "John, I'm so sorry. I had no idea."

"It was a few days ago now," he replied, well aware that he was being stiff and formal but unable to find a way to relax, "so... I mean, it's over, I guess. It's all sorted."

"And you're here alone?"

"It's not so bad."

"Sure, but..." She paused, clearly concerned. "You're in this house all by yourself?"

"I'm not worried about ghosts, if that's what you mean."

"No, but still, it doesn't seem..." She paused again. "Well, it just seems kind of morbid, that's all. What about your father?"

"He's coming for the funeral."

"Oh, that's nice of him," she said sarcastically. "Still gunning for that father of the year award, I take it."

"I don't need him here." He winced a little as he felt his toe hurting again. The nail felt loose, so he figured he'd have to rip it off later. The strange thing was, he couldn't quite remember how he'd hurt it in the first place.

"No, but you need someone. Jesus, it's a complete coincidence that I just happened to drop by today, and now I find you all alone in the house where you found a dead body just a few days ago. I mean, I know your grandmother wasn't exactly... I don't want to say bad things about dead people, but I know what it was like for you, living with her. Still, this must have been a huge shock."

"I -"

Before he could finish, she stepped closer and put her arms around him, giving him a tight hug that momentarily pressed their bodies together. Her fingers pressed against the back of his t-shirt, rubbing against the burn marks from his grandmother's cigarettes, but not enough for him to flinch. Instead, he put his arms around her in return, even though he felt uncomfortable being so close.

"Don't squeeze me too tight," she told him. "I'm still scarred. I've only been out of hospital for a month."

"How did it go?"

"Fine, can't you tell? I'm stiff as a board, can't bend at all. Turns out, screwing a metal pole into my back *did* help with the scoliosis."

"Does it hurt?"

"Like a bitch." Taking a step back, she turned and suddenly hoisted her shirt up, exposing the thick, fresh scar that ran all the way up her back, with stitches still holding the edges of flesh together. "A two-foot titanium pole," she explained, "has literally been screwed to my spine. Remember last time you saw me, when I was all curled over like an old toenail. And now look at me, I've got the posture of a queen. Go on, touch it."

"I..." Staring at her stitches, he felt a shiver pass through his body. "No, I'm fine."

"Touch it," she said again. "I'll be totally offended if you don't."

Realizing that had couldn't argue, he reached out and let his fingers brush against the stitches. For a moment, he was tempted to pull on them, to unravel her back and open the scar up to see her spine, but a few seconds later he was distracted as one of his fingers nudged her bare, cold flesh.

"Everyone's mega impressed," she continued, pulling her t-shirt down and turning to him, before pausing as she stared into his eyes. "You're not okay, John."

"I'm not?"

"You can't *possibly* be okay," she continued. "No-one could be okay in your situation. You don't have to believe in ghosts to find the whole thing freaky. What have you been doing the past few days?"

"Cleaning," he said cautiously. "Tidying."

"And your Dad still sends money?"

"It's his house," John pointed out. "He bought it for Gran and me to live in after my mother died, remember? He sends money to my account each month for living expenses. He's doing well out there, money isn't a problem."

"But you're not *living*, are you?" she replied. "Not really. I mean, hell, I can't even walk without pain, and I probably get about more than you do." Stepping past him, she looked around the room for a moment before turning to him again. "There's a ghost in this house."

"There is?"

She nodded.

"How..." He paused. "How can you tell?"

"It's obvious."

"It is?"

She turned to him. "There's a ghost in this house and its name is John Myers."

He sighed. "I'm not -"

"Let's get out of here."

He frowned.

"Have you even left the house in the past

few days?" she continued. "I don't mean for groceries, forget that, have you actually gone out anywhere? I know since we finished school you've been kind of spending a lot of time in your own company, developing your reputation as a hermit. Be honest, have you done *anything* recently? Do you even bother to keep up with the few people who're still knocking about in this dull old town?"

He paused. "You're... Actually, you're kind of the first person I've seen since... Well, since it all happened. Apart from the guy who works in the petrol station where I buy food, but I think he's starting to think I'm weird, since I kind of go in there every night now. I like to go late when there's less chance of anyone else being there."

"Sounds mentally and emotionally healthy," she replied, taking his hand and starting to lead him to the door. "Come on, it's my duty as your friend to get you out of here and remind you that the rest of the world exists. Just don't mock the way I walk. It's better than before when I was all curled up, right?"

***

"So university is kind of slightly soul-destroying," she said a little while later as they walked along the windy promenade, with a strong breeze blowing in from the sea. "The only way to get by is to drink heavily, and I mean *heavily*. Turns out, I have some kind of limit that keeps me from getting blind drunk, so I usually don't last the whole night. Not that it's not fun, though. You should totally apply and go next year 'cause, you know, it'd better than withering away like you're doing now."

"Sure."

"Maybe you could even come to Peterborough. Oh my God, that would be so cool, we could be housemates!"

"Sure. Maybe."

"Does that mean you might actually do it?" she asked. "I know you said you were taking a gap year, but you're blatantly not planning to do anything fun. When people take a gap year, they usually go traveling or they take a job for experience, something like that. They don't just sit around the house doing nothing." She waited for a reply. "You'll be fine, you know. Uni isn't that terrifying. You'll make friends once you get out into the world."

"I have friends."

"You *had* friends. At school. And how many of them do you still see?"

"Not many."

"Only the ones who really make an effort. Which probably means just me."

He allowed himself a faint smile. "The important ones, then."

"And let me guess. That old witch told you

there's no point trying to make more friends, didn't she?"

"She just said I should be realistic about my personality. I'm just not very outgoing."

"Rubbish."

"She had a point."

"It's a self-fulfilling prophecy. Once you start believing it, it becomes true. Fortunately, the reverse is also true. Stop believing in it, it stops becoming true."

"Maybe."

"So what are you going to do now?" She nudged his arm playfully. "Come on, dude, you're free! I know how your grandmother held you back, so what's the plan for the first day of the rest of your life?"

"In general?" He paused, genuinely stumped by the question. "I don't know."

"Sit around in that house, listening to bumps in the night, rotting away?"

He shook his head.

"I'm scared that's exactly what you'll do," she told him. "I remember a few years ago, you were full of ambition about becoming some big writer, and then slowly she..." She paused. "You mustn't let your grandmother ruin things for you. I know she said some pretty cruel things to you, I feel like she chipped away at your soul until there's pretty much nothing left. I mean, it's too bad you didn't rebel and fight back, but none of that matters now. You don't have an ounce of confidence, do you?"

"It wasn't that bad," he replied. "I can't blame her."

"She was wrong, you know. You totally *can* be a writer, you can be anything you want. You just need to find your voice, and you need to get out and actually meet people." She nudged his arm again. "I believe in you."

"It's just a pipe-dream. It's not realistic or -"

Hurrying a couple of steps ahead, she stopped, then she turned to face him and grabbed him by the shoulders. "Not another word of that," she said firmly, albeit with a faint smile. "Jonathan Myers, you are damn well not going to let a vindictive old bitch drag you down, especially now she's out of your life. And yes, I'm aware that I just broke my own rule about nice things and dead people, but I don't care. The truth is coming. Are you ready for it?"

"Alison -"

"Your grandmother was a horrible, horrible woman. She was a mean, cruel, vindictive old bitch who tried to ruin your life for reasons that, frankly, we don't even need to try to understand anymore, because she's gone. And to be honest, when you told me she'd keeled over earlier, my first thought was that it's about time. You have your whole life ahead of you, John, and that's a good thing. You have to live it."

"I will."

"Uh-huh, and pigs might fly." She stared at him for a moment, before letting go of his shoulders and starting to walk again. "Well, I'm not going to give up on you, you idiot. I'm going to badger you for as long as it takes, and then I'll badger you some more. I care about you, you bloody idiot, and I won't let you fade away like some kind of ghost."

CHAPTER ELEVEN

Today

STOPPING AT THE FRONT DOOR, John took a moment to fumble through his pockets for the key. He'd been so focused on his own thoughts during the walk back to the house after leaving the book club meeting, he'd forgotten to be nervous. Now, close to midnight, he unlocked the door and stepped into the hallway, and as he did so he realized the fear had left him. The darkness of the house held no more terror, and he wasn't sure whether to feel relieved that he'd overcome it all or angry that he'd let the place dog his thoughts for so long.

Smiling, he turned to shut the door...

And found Hannah standing right behind him.

"Hey," she said cautiously.

He stared, blinking a couple of times as if he expected her to vanish in a puff of smoke.

"So..." She paused. "I followed you. Is that totally awful?"

"You followed me all the way from the flat... to here?"

She winced slightly, as if the idea was excruciatingly embarrassing, before silently mouthing the word 'Sorry'.

"It's late," he told her, even though he couldn't deny that her presence was... positive, in some way he didn't want to acknowledge just yet. Positive and definitely flattering for a man in his late thirties. "I'm sorry, *why* did you follow me?"

"Is this the house?" she asked.

"What house?"

"The one you talked about. The one that's haunted."

"I..."

"Or *not* haunted, as you actually said." She peered past him, looking at the stairs. "It doesn't look much like a haunted house. It looks like a totally normal house."

"Aren't all houses normal?" he asked.

"Oh no," she replied, suddenly stepping inside and heading over to look up at the landing. "I've studied haunting cases online, and some houses you can just tell by looking at them, they're haunted. It's a very definite quality that some of them just exude. I know that doesn't sound very scientific, but it's true, after a while you just develop a kind of sixth sense about the whole thing. Some houses give off a clear vibe that just seems to let you know there's something dark and nasty hiding inside. This one, not so much." She turned to him again. "It just looks *so* ordinary. So normal." She paused, before frowning. "Then again, maybe that's just what the house *wants* us to think."

"I..." Pausing, with the door still open, he realized that he didn't quite have the resolve to ask her to leave, at least not yet. Besides, even though he was a married man, he told himself there was no reason why he shouldn't spend a little more time with someone who was clearly so interested in his work. Slowly, trying not to feel guilty, he pushed the door shut. "I'm afraid I don't have anything to offer you," he told her. "No wine, no -"

"Ta-da!" She pulled a bottle of red wine from the satchel slung over her shoulder. "It was Gary's actually, I purloined it from his flat, but he won't mind. Well, he will, but he'll get over it."

"Right." He paused again, feeling a little uncomfortable. "I don't have a bottle opener or -"

"Oh, I do," she said quickly, interrupting him as she pulled an opener from her satchel. "I don't have glasses, but we can just drink from the bottle." She waited for him to reply. "I know this is totally intrusive, and I can leave if you want, and I swear I'm not some kind of crazy stalker fan, I just.. You're cool. You're one of my favorite authors, and you're right here in town, in a haunted house, and I'd be crazy not to want to come and hang out. If I didn't at least try, I'd probably literally regret it for the rest of my life." She waited for him to answer. "But I can totally leave if you're uncomfortable."

"Not at all," he replied, taking a deep breath. "You... How old are you, if you don't mind me asking?"

"Twenty-one."

"You seem younger."

"Thanks."

"Oh, I didn't -"

"So you don't think this place is haunted, huh?" she continued with a smile, slipping past him and heading into the front room. Despite all her talk of being willing to leave, she seemed confident enough to take charge of the situation. "What happened? Did someone die here or something?"

His first instinct was to not tell her any more than she already knew, but at the same time he felt moved to open up a little. "My grandmother."

"When?"

"A long time ago. Back in the days when I still lived here."

She wedged the wine bottle under her legs and began to twist the screw into the cork. "So it might be your grandmother's spirit that's knocking about the place, huh? And from what you said earlier, I get the feeling that you're trying to prove something by staying here tonight."

"I guess so."

"Like a personal victory, like you not only need to test to see if her ghost is here, but you also need to prove to yourself that you've got the balls." With the bottle held firmly between her thighs, she was struggling to get the cork out.

"You're very perceptive."

"So do you need to be alone for that," she gasped, still struggling, "or is company okay?"

He knew he should really be alone, but as Hannah pulled the cork out and almost dropped the bottle, he couldn't bring himself to ask her to leave. "I don't mind company."

"I spilled a little," she pointed out, looking down at a few splashes of wine on the carpet.

"I don't care."

She pulled the bottle from between her legs and took a glug, before passing it to him. "So how did she die? And where?"

"Aneurysm, I think," he replied, taking a sip. "And she died in one of the bedrooms upstairs."

"What kind of aneurysm?"

"I... I don't remember."

"And you found her?"

He nodded.

"That must have been creepy as hell."

"It had its moments."

She took the wine bottle back and took another, longer sip, swallowing several times before handing it back to him. "Almost enough to make a guy go a little weird," she said with a knowing smile, as a dribble of wine ran down her chin and onto her neck.

"Almost," he admitted.

"And to make a guy who's already weird, go even weirder."

He smiled.

"Huh," she continued, "well, we'll get to that in a minute. Whether you're aware of it or not, you most likely have a great deal of troubled psychic energy stored up in your soul. Troubled energy isn't necessarily bad, because it can be turned into a positive force, but you have to understand its shape and form before you can start to manipulate it, otherwise it sits in your mind and rots, and then the rot spreads. That's what rot does." She turned to look around the room, before glancing back at him. "I have experience with it comes to contacting the dead, you know."

He frowned. "You do?"

"I've been on several overnight trips to haunted houses," she continued, "and I've both assisted with and led attempts to establish communications with restless spirits. I have a training certificate from Marc X. Martell, have you heard of him?"

He shook his head.

"Well, I have a training certificate from his online school, which mean I know what I'm doing when it comes to this type of thing. I don't have my equipment with me, obviously, but I personally believe myself to be very well attuned to the energy of the supernatural world. If there's a ghost here, I think I'll be able to sense it."

"Is that right?"

"If you want it to be sensed, that is."

"I..." Pausing, he realized that the night was rapidly running away from him, and that his plan to spend a calm, quiet few hours in bed was starting to become something much more dramatic and theatrical. Still, an amateur séance seemed like as good a way as any to finish off his last night in the house and to prove beyond a shadow of a doubt that there was no ghost. "Do your best," he said finally, with a smile. "I've never actually been involved with anything like that before."

"Seriously? Never?"

He shook his head.

"Well, then tonight's your lucky night," she continued, heading past him again and making her way into the kitchen. "You're so fortunate that I'm here. Oh my God, is that a hatch on the floor?"

"It leads to the basement."

"Can we go and look?"

"Later. Maybe I should show you the room where she died first."

"Totally," she continued, hurrying to the stairs and immediately starting to head up to the landing. "Don't worry, I won't tell anyone about anything that happens here tonight. It'll just be between the two of us, I won't even blog about it."

"That's good," he replied, taking another swig of wine before following her up. "I think I'd rather keep it that way."

CHAPTER TWELVE

Twenty years ago

"DO YOU MIND IF I CRASH HERE TONIGHT?" Alison asked, yawning as she crushed a beer can in her fist and then set it on the table with all the others. "I'm too tired to walk home. My back's killing me. Sorry to play the cripple card for sympathy, but it's true."

"Sure," John replied, having anticipated the question for a while – and having hoped that it would come. They'd spent the evening watching DVDs, but it was almost 4am now and they were both starting to flag. Still, it had been good to hang out with Alison again after months without seeing her, and he was starting to realize that he could be sociable after all, so long as he felt comfortable.

Grabbing the remote, he switched the TV off.

"I've got to go all the way back up to Peterborough tomorrow," she muttered, wincing slightly as she hauled herself out of the armchair. "Damn it, I feel like an old woman sometimes. I swear to God, I'm starting to get one of those weak bone diseases, whatever they're called." Stretching her arms, she turned to him and smiled. "My boyfriend back at uni thinks I'm going to become a premature old woman. Like I'll be gray-haired and knitting by the time I'm thirty. The sad part is, I could totally see that happening."

"I'm sure you'll be fine," he replied, getting to his feet. "You can take my bed and I'll sleep on the sofa."

"I'll take your grandmother's room," she told him, turning and heading to the door before stopping and glancing back at him. "Oh. If that's okay, I mean. I don't want to step on any toes or do anything weird."

He stared at her for a moment, before realizing that there was no reason to argue with her. "It's fine," he said with a faint, not-entirely-successful smile. "I should find you some clean sheets, though."

"Haven't you changed them since she died?" she asked with a laugh, before raising both eyebrows in shock. "You *haven't*? That's gross, John!"

"I didn't get around to it."

"We've got to knock those weird kinks out of you," she continued, heading to the hallway and then upstairs. "No offense, but you can change your grandmother's old sheets yourself. Unless you want to sleep in there and I'll take *your* bed?" She paused. "Actually, that probably wouldn't be much better."

***

Alison, it turned out, snored like a foghorn. On his back in bed and wide awake, John listened to the sound of her snores drifting along the landing from the other bedroom, and although he was a little frustrated at being kept up, he couldn't help but feel just a little impressed. After all, Alison had a fairly small build so it was somewhat surprising that she was capable of making a sound like an angry donkey.

Besides, any sound was better than silence. Silence always made him worry about what might come next.

Unable to sleep, he began to run through the day's events in his mind, trying to work out – as usual, when it came to Alison – whether she'd been giving him any signals he might have missed. He wasn't in love with her, he knew that, but he couldn't deny that she was attractive, and he was starting to think that he needed to sleep with a girl, any girl, just to get his first time over with. Alison was a friend and would clearly never be anything more, but friends could still help each other out. He just didn't know how to bring the possibility up without risking what they had.

Suddenly, he realized that the snoring had stopped. He allowed himself a faint smile, rolled onto his side and closed his eyes, figuring that he should probably try to get to sleep during what might be a brief window. Even though the house was silent now, he was glad to know that someone else was nearby, and he couldn't help but feel grateful that she'd shown up to visit. Ever since she'd gone away to university, they'd spoken a few times by email but it hadn't really been like the old days. Now, at least, she was showing that she hadn't forgotten him. Drifting into dreams, he allowed himself to start thinking about other things.

"Hey," he heard Alison whisper suddenly, from behind him, "do you mind if I get in?"

He opened his eyes, staring into darkness as he felt the bed creak and dip slightly. She was crawling under the duvet, and a moment later he felt her bare leg against his. He froze, terrified and hopeful at the same time, and then he felt her hand reach around and rest on his waist, while she pressed her body gently against his back. He couldn't tell whether she was naked, but he told himself that there was no way she'd get into bed with him if she didn't want something to happen. Still frozen with fear, he ran through all his possible options before reminding himself that Alison was no idiot: she had to understand that he'd start to get ideas, so he felt certain now that she was at least giving him the opportunity to make a move. All he had to do was roll to face her and do... something.

Anything.

He opened his mouth, but no words came out. Slowly he rolled onto his back, before lifting the duvet and looking down to see her arm resting on his bare waist. The sight was strangely comforting, and he couldn't help thinking that it would be nice to sleep with someone on a regular basis. After a moment, however, he realized that something seemed wrong, and as his eyes adjusted a little to the darkness he saw that her hand was wrinkled and old, with prominent, swollen veins running through the skin. A shiver passed through his chest as he realized that he recognized the hand, but he told himself he was wrong, that his mind was playing tricks on him and that all he had to do was look at her face and he'd see that everything was okay. Either that, or he was dreaming.

"Alison?" he whispered, his voice tense with fear.

He waited.

Silence.

Slowly, he turned to look at her. The room

was too dark for him to see properly, and at first all he could make out was the general shape of her head on the next pillow, just ten inches or so from his face. He opened his mouth to say her name again, but gradually he began to make out her features, and as his eyes adjusted more he was able to just about discern two wide-open eyes staring straight at him, becoming more visible with each passing second.

His grandmother.

"No!" he shouted, pulling back and tumbling off the side of the bed, landing hard on the carpet but immediately rolling away until he slammed into the radiator. He heard footsteps in the darkness, and a moment later the light flickered on to reveal Alison standing in the doorway, startled and staring at him with shock in her eyes.

"What's wrong?" she asked, looking around the room. "John?"

He turned to the bed, but there was no sign of anyone. Where his grandmother had been just a moment ago, now the duvet was undisturbed.

"You scared the hell out of me." Hurrying over to him, Alison dropped down onto her knees and took hold of him by the shoulders. "You were calling out. What happened?"

"Did you..." He stared at the bed for a moment longer, before turning to her. He could tell she had no idea what had happened, which meant he must have dreamed the whole thing. "Nothing," he told her, getting to his feet and starting to feel like a complete fool. Try as he might to tell himself that there had been nothing with him a moment ago, however, he could still feel the touch of his grandmother's arm around his waist. "It was nothing," he added finally, turning to Alison and trying his best to seem calm. "Really. Nothing happened."

"And you still want to tell me that you're dealing with this okay?"

"I am!"

"Apart from waking up screaming?"

"It was just one time."

"And what's wrong with your back?" she asked, stepping past him and grabbing his shoulder so she could get a better look. "Jesus Christ, John, where did all these burn marks come from?"

"It doesn't matter."

"Some of them..." She paused. "John, some of these look really new, like they just happened a few minutes ago."

He pulled away. "You don't know what you're talking about."

She stared at him for a moment, clearly not convinced, and this time there was a hint of pity in her eyes. "John..."

"Maybe you should go."

"What?"

"It's almost six," he continued, "so there's not much point sleeping anymore. You said you have to go back to Peterborough today, so..." He paused, feeling a shiver pass through his body as he realized that he just wanted her to leave. "I'm fine," he added, spotting a cigarette on the nightstand. "Everyone has nightmares, and that's all it was. You don't need to worry about me. Nothing bad is going to happen."

CHAPTER THIRTEEN

Today

"DO YOU FEEL ANYTHING?" Hannah whispered, as they sat on the floor in the dark nursery with their backs against the wall, watching the spot where twenty years earlier John had found his grandmother's body. "Anything at all?"

He paused. "Um... No. Sorry. What about you?"

She looked around the room for a moment, wide-eyed with wonder. "Not yet."

"So -"

"But I think it's coming."

He frowned. "I'm sorry?"

"I think there's some kind of unusual energy in the place," she continued, taking another sip of wine before handing the bottle back to him. She wiped a red bead from her bottom lip. "It's hard to express the feeling in words, it's more like a kind of vibration running through my body. There's nothing here now, but... There *has* been, I just don't know when." She reached a hand out and swirled it through the air. "This space has been disturbed in recent times by some kind of dark energy, something that left a trace. There's been an entity here, maybe even in this very room, and it'll return soon."

"It will, huh?" he replied. "Well, I'm not sure how you'd go about measuring or proving something like that."

"Proof is for when you want other people to believe you," she replied, turning to him with a smile. "I'm more interested in personal understanding. If *I* know something, then that's all that matters. I know other people will catch up eventually. By the way, do you have a cigarette I can nick?"

"A..." He frowned. "Um, no. Sorry."

"I thought I saw there was a packet in your coat pocket earlier."

He shook his head. "You must be mistaken."

"Huh." She stared at him for a moment longer, before turning to look at the opposite wall. "Is that where the body was?"

He nodded.

"And then you dragged her onto the bed?"

"I just thought... I don't really know why I did that."

"Maybe you were panicking. You were all alone, right?"

He nodded again.

"That must have been hard." She put a hand on his arm, as if to reassure him. "Then what did you do?"

"I checked to see if she was really dead."

"And she was?"

He nodded.

"And then what?"

He swallowed hard, fully aware that her hand was still resting on his arm. "And then I called for an ambulance."

She stared at him for a moment, her face just about visible in the darkness thanks to a patch of moonlight that had fallen across one of the walls. "And then what?"

"And then... It's all kind of a blur."

"It must have been hard for you."

"I was fine."

"What kind of woman was she?"

He paused. "A tyrant," he said finally.

"Seriously?"

"She was a bitter old woman. Vindictive, cruel... Not just to me, this isn't self-pity. She was well known for having a harsh temper, and for turning against people. She was worse at home, though. Behind closed doors, she really turned the screws. To be honest, if she hadn't died, I'd probably still be under her thumb."

"You were a Granny's boy, huh?"

"For some reason, I just didn't have the urge to rebel."

She stared at him for a moment. "I find that very hard to believe," she said finally. "*Very* hard."

"She told me once that I'd never be a writer. She said I didn't have that kind of mind, that I should stop dreaming and just focus on something more practical. She used to say the same thing to my mother when she was younger too, and it worked on her. She wasn't lucky like me, she didn't get to escape."

"Your mother was a writer?"

"She wanted to be," he continued, "but my grandmother ground her down. It was my mother who had real talent, I'm just a hack."

"I don't think you're a hack," she told him.

"You're biased."

"Why?"

He turned to her. "Never mind. My mother wrote a lot of short stories. She even finished a novel, I think, but it all got lost."

"You didn't save it?"

"My grandmother burned everything."

"I'm sorry," Hanna replied, watching his

expression carefully for a moment. "What happened to her?"

"My mother?" He paused. "One day, when I was very young, she locked herself in the bathroom and drank half a bottle of bleach. My grandmother broke the door down when she heard the cries, but it was too late. My mother died in agonizing pain, and I..." His gaze flickered for a moment, as if the memory was too much. "I heard her screams. In some ways, I don't think I've stopped hearing them since."

"No-one should have to hear something like that."

"I read up on it later," he continued. "The bleach would have burned through her gut and -"

"Maybe you don't need to think about all that."

"It would've burned her esophagus too. All the way down into her stomach, it would have just eaten through the lining. Her stomach acid would have burst out too, spreading to the rest of her body. I've researched death a lot for my novels, in some ways I think I've been searching to find a more painful method of death, and I've come up with nothing." He sighed. "And since my father already lived on the other side of the world by that point, I ended up living with my grandmother."

They sat in silence for a moment.

"Sucks to be you, huh?" Hannah said finally.

"I'm lucky," he continued. "I'm still here."

"You don't have a lighter, do you?"

He turned to her.

"A cigarette lighter?" she asked.

"No. Why?"

"I could just use one, that's all." She grabbed the corkscrew she'd used on the wine bottle, and slipped it into her pocket. "Sorry, thinking several steps ahead, that's all."

"I don't even know why I've told you all of this," he continued. "I haven't even told my wife the whole story."

"You should."

He nodded.

"I'm definitely picking something up," she added, crawling forward toward the center of the room, until she was just a couple of feet from the spot where, years ago, the stain had been left on the carpet. "Don't worry, I don't think anything's going to start banging on the doors and windows, but I definitely feel a presence. There's something in the house with us. I don't know if it's a ghost, though. It feels like some other kind of entity, but I guess I could be wrong. There's definitely something here."

"There is, huh?"

"But it's not *here*. It's not in this room."

"I'm pretty sure this room is *exactly* where it'd be," he replied.

She shook her head.

"You think you know better than me?" he asked. "She died in here, right over there against that wall."

"I still don't think the presence is focused here. I think it's elsewhere in the house. In fact, this feels like one of the least affected rooms."

"Okay," he replied, starting to see through her act. "If you say so."

She smiled. "You don't believe me."

"I believe you, I just..." Pausing, he realized that she was right: even though he *wanted* to believe what she was saying, he couldn't quite bring himself to accept that the house was haunted. If they'd met just twenty-four hours earlier, things might have been different, but now he felt totally at peace with the place and ready to move on. He liked Hannah, but he'd already written her off as an over-enthusiastic wannabe ghost chaser who'd spent too much time online. "Maybe it's best to leave these things alone," he said finally. "If there's a presence here, that's okay, let it be here."

She shook her head.

"No?" he continued.

"If there's a presence here," she replied, "that means it wants something. Can you think of anything your grandmother might consider to be unfinished business?"

"Nothing."

"Maybe she just wants to put more burns on

your back."

"The -" He paused, suddenly starting to worry. "How did you know about that?"

"I'm very observant."

"Still, how -"

"There's definitely *something* that keeps her here," she continued, interrupting him, before turning and looking at the door. She paused for a moment. "Did you hear that?"

"Hear what?"

"I thought..." She paused again. "It was probably just the wind."

Setting the bottle of wine down, he crawled over to join her in the center of the room, looking out at the landing. For a moment, he listened to the extreme silence of the house. Of all the houses he'd ever spent time in, the house on Everley Street was perhaps the most silent of all.

"Are you holding your breath too?" Hannah whispered.

"I am."

"I just thought I heard a scratching sound," she continued, "that's all."

"Coming from where?"

"I don't know. Downstairs, maybe."

"Could it be badgers?"

She turned to him. "Badgers?"

"Nasty little things," he continued with a smile. "If there's a badger in the house, we're in trouble."

She laughed, breaking the hush. "Don't talk to me about badgers," she said finally. "Trust me, I could tell you some war stories involving badgers that'd turn your hair gray."

"I'm serious," he told her. She had a nice laugh, and he wanted to hear it again. "If it's a choice between a badger or a ghost, I'd rather face a ghost, because a badger can cause some serious damage when it's angry and -"

He stopped suddenly as they both heard a loud, heavy bump from downstairs, as if a wooden surface was being briefly but violently shaken. Whatever caused it, it was quick and over in just a couple of seconds, but John and Hannah stayed completely silent for a moment before slowly turning to one another.

"It's definitely downstairs," Hannah whispered, slowly getting to her feet. "I was right."

Hauling himself up and following her to the door, John could feel his heart pounding as he waited for another bump. He wanted to tell her that she was wrong, that she was imagining the whole thing, but at the same time he knew he couldn't write off the sound so easily.

"We have to go see," Hannah told him.

"It might be a burglar."

"We still have to go see," she replied, taking a step out onto the landing. "Don't worry if it's a burglar, we'll just beat the living hell out of him."

"But -"

"We *have* to go and see." Come on, don't disappoint me. Don't be a coward.

"But -" Realizing that she was right, John followed her to the top of the stairs. He'd been so caught up in the relief of realizing the house wasn't haunted, it had never occurred to him that they might actually hear something. He still wasn't willing to accept that there might be a ghost after all, but he knew that the banging sound had been real, and he could see the fear in Hannah's eyes as she looked down toward the hallway.

Fear and excitement.

"Hello?" she called out suddenly, before turning to him. "It's good to try establishing contact if there's a spirit around. Plus, it's only polite. And if there's a burglar, hopefully he'll leave without us having to beat him to a pulp."

"It was probably just..." John's voice trailed off as he realized that he couldn't come up with a feasible explanation, even though he was certain there must be one. He was tempted to make another badger joke, but the moment didn't feel right.

Slowly, Hannah began to make her way downstairs, with John close behind.

"Hello?" she said again. "Is anyone here?"

"Wait," John said, suddenly pushing past her as he realized that he couldn't let her go first, not if there was even a chance that something dangerous was in the house. Reaching the hallway, he looked around, but there was no sign of anyone. "It's okay," he continued, turning to Hannah, "I think -"

Suddenly there was another bang, and this time they could both tell it was coming from the kitchen.

"That's not a badger," Hannah hissed, hurrying past him and then stopping in the doorway, "I think it came from..." She paused, her eyes filled with shock before finally she turned to him. "I think it came from the basement."

CHAPTER FOURTEEN

Twenty years ago

"DAMN IT," JOHN MUTTERED as he pulled on the edge of the carpet, only to find that it still wouldn't come up. He'd spent the past hour or so picking out every tack he could find, but still one seemed to have eluded him. Grabbing the hammer, he began to search once again, before finally spotting the offending culprit. After picking it out, he dropped the hammer and pulled on the carpet again, and at last he was able to start ripping it up from the floor.

He worked hard and fast, gutting the room completely. He knew that his father would eventually show up to visit, and the last thing he wanted at that point was to still be living in a house filled with reminders of his grandmother, so following Alison's departure earlier that morning he'd decided to start clearing everything out. He'd started with his grandmother's old room, naturally, and he'd hauled the bed and all the other furniture out to other rooms so he could get to the carpet. He had no real plan in mind, other than the absolute determination to make the place as empty as possible.

Just as he was pulling the carpet through the doorway and out onto the landing, he heard the phone ringing. His first instinct was to ignore it, but finally he dropped the carpet and headed to his bedroom, figuring that while few people ever called him, the ones who *did* call tended to have a good reason.

"Hello?" he said as he picked up the receiver.

"Jonathan?"

He immediately recognized the voice and wished he'd let the phone keep ringing.

"Hi, Dorothy," he said, trying to sound polite. For a moment, he stared down at the cigarette stub on the nightstand. "I don't know if -"

"I heard the awful news," she continued. "Gladys told me at the last fuchsia meeting. Everyone's so completely shocked, your grandmother seemed so full of life just last week."

"It was a surprise," he replied, wiping sweat

from his brow.

"I was just wondering, dear, if you know when the funeral will be taking place? A few of us would so very much like to attend the service, and there's also the small matter of flowers to arrange."

"I..." He paused for a moment, imagining all his grandmother's friends showing up at the church. "I don't know yet," he told her finally. "It's still being arranged, it's very complicated."

"Complicated?"

"I'll let you know as soon as I can."

"If you would, dear. Do you know where it'll be? I hope it's somewhere close to the center of town, most of us are a little unsteady on our feet these days."

He paused again. "Actually, she always said she wanted to be buried in Essex."

"Essex?"

"Where she was born."

"Oh." There was silence on the other end of the line for a moment. "Well, yes, I suppose I can understand that, but... Will there be no service here in Bournemouth at all?"

"I'm still not sure. I need to talk to my father about it, but he lives in Australia so it's not easy getting in touch with him."

"When is he flying in?" she asked. "I'd like to pay my condolences in person."

"He won't be coming for the funeral."

"I beg your pardon?"

"He let me know last night," John continued, surprised by how quickly he was able to come up with answers that sounded believable. "He has too much work to do, so he can't make it. He and my grandmother were never very close anyway, so I understand. He's going to come and visit soon, though."

"So are you making all the arrangements yourself?"

"I've got some help," he told her. "A friend of mine was here yesterday, and she's going to give me a hand."

"Oh." Another pause. "Well, I do hope you decide to hold *some* kind of service here in Bournemouth. Your grandmother was a highly respected member of the local community, you know. She was a very popular woman."

"I know," he replied, unable to stifle a faint smile. "Is there anything else I can help you with?"

"Well... No, I suppose -"

"I'll call you when I know about the funeral," he added, interrupting her. "Have a nice day."

Setting the phone down, he paused for a moment, feeling his heart pounding in his chest. He'd known for a few days now that he'd have to start letting people know about the funeral, but the whole thing just felt too huge to deal with. At least he figured he'd managed to get the league of old ladies out of the way, which was one of the bigger hurdles he was facing, but there were going to be other people calling and he knew it would be difficult to dissuade them all from showing up or asking more questions

Hearing a noise downstairs, he headed out onto the landing and saw a fresh batch of mail down on the mat. Making his way down to take a look, he picked up the letters and found that they were all addressed to his grandmother. He wondered how long it would take before they stopped coming, although he figured that he'd need to contact a few companies and explain the situation. Still, that was a job for another day. For now, he had to focus on getting everything out of the house.

And he needed to set things on fire.

***

"Are you in there?" a voice called out from nearby, barely audible over the roar of the flames. "Hello? Jonathan?"

Turning, John saw the garden gate opening, and a moment later Mr. Shepherd from the next house appeared through the thick black smoke that was filling the air.

"Hello, Mr. Shepherd," John said with a polite smile. Getting up from the white plastic patio chair, he headed over to shake the man's hand. "I hope the smoke isn't bothering you."

"Bothering me?" Mr. Shepherd stared for a moment at the inferno in the center of the garden. Carpets, curtains, cushions, clothes, items of bed linen, even items of furniture had been stacked up in a huge pile and set alight, and a column of black smoke was rising up, visible no doubt for miles around. "You can't have a bonfire like this," he continued. "You're lucky no-one's reported you to the council!"

"What's wrong?" John asked, watching as flames tore through some of his grandmother's most treasured possessions, which had turned out to be surprisingly flammable. "I'm just burning things."

"For one thing," Mr. Shepherd replied, "all that ash is going to fall on my garden. For another, Mrs. Henderson down the road put some washing out earlier, and now she'll have to do it all again."

"Oh," John said with a frown. Turning, he looked toward one of the distant gardens and saw some white clothes on a line. "Sorry, I didn't think about any of that."

"Not to mention what this is doing to the environment. If you want to get rid of this amount of household waste, you're supposed to call the council and arrange a special pick-up."

"I didn't want to bother them. It's not really a huge fire, is it?"

"It's big enough," Mr. Shepherd said, shielding his face from the heat as he took a step back. "Is your father around?"

John shook his head.

"So it's just you, now that your grandmother has passed?"

"Just me," John said calmly. He usually panicked when he was talking to people, but this time he felt strangely comfortable.

"And..." Mr. Shepherd paused for a moment, as if he wasn't quite sure what to say next. "I mean, what are you... What are you going to do?"

"Technically my father owns the house," John pointed out, "so it's really up to him."

"Huh. And what about the funeral?"

"Essex."

"I'm sorry."

"She wanted to be buried in Essex," he explained, "so I'm going to have to arrange that. I'm not quite sure where to start, but I'm going to go to the funeral home tomorrow morning and see what they can do to help. Hopefully it'll be as simple as making a few phone calls and then getting her body driven or flown over there. I don't suppose I can just carry her onto a train."

"Right," Mr. Shepherd said with a frown. "So there won't be any kind of service here in Bournemouth?"

"I'm afraid not. If you'd like to come to

Essex, though, you're more than welcome."

"I... Well, no, I don't think I'll be able to make it. If you could let me know the details, though, I'd be happy to send some flowers."

"I'll make sure to do that," John told him. "Have a nice day, Mr. Shepherd. Good luck with your garden. I noticed from one of the windows that it's looking really good this year. I hope you manage to fix the problem with your compost system. Are the rats still bothering you?"

He rolled his eyes. "Kill one, two pop up in its place."

"I'm sure you'll win out eventually."

"Huh," the older man muttered, clearly unimpressed but apparently unwilling to push the matter too far. "You're going through a tough time, kid," he added, taking a step back. "Just... I don't know, try not to have any more big fires, okay? It's disruptive to the whole neighborhood. You really should've thought about that before you started."

"Sorry," John replied, watching as Mr. Shepherd left. He felt bad for causing a problem and he didn't like the fact that he'd been 'told off', albeit mildly; still, turning back to look at the fire, he couldn't help but feel relieved that he was getting rid of his grandmother's possessions. Once they were all gone, he'd feel less like she was still around the house, so he headed back inside to grab another section of carpet. Hauling it into the garden, he heaved it onto the bonfire, and within seconds the flames had taken hold, sending another plume of thick black smoke high into the afternoon sky.

CHAPTER FIFTEEN

Today

"WAIT!" JOHN CALLED OUT, sitting up in bed and blinking as harsh morning sunlight streamed through the window. Hearing another knock at the front door, he grabbed his clothes from the floor and began to get dressed while heading out onto the landing.

Looking down toward the hallway, he realized he could see figures on the other side of the front door's frosted glass. He frowned, trying to work out who could possibly be out there, but a moment later there was another knock and he realized that whoever it was, they clearly weren't going to go away.

"I'm coming!" he shouted, finishing getting

dressed before hurrying down the stairs. He'd been fast asleep until a moment ago, and as he unlocked the door and pulled it open, he felt strangely tired and a little out of sorts. "Sorry," he muttered, "I just -"

He froze as soon as he saw his wife smiling at him.

"Is this it?" asked Scott, his ten-year-old son, scrunching his nose up as he peered into the house. "It's so small!"

"What are you doing here?" John asked, startled by their sudden arrival.

"Pleased to see you too, honey," Sarah said, ushering Scott and Katie inside before stepping through the doorway and planting a kiss on her husband's cheek. "Call me paranoid, but when you told me last night that you were at a fan event talking about your books, I started to worry that you'd suffered some kind of stroke, so I called Reginald and forced him to tell me what you were up to, then I bundled the kids into the car and now..." She paused for a moment, biting her bottom lip. "Why the hell didn't you tell me that you were coming back to your childhood home?"

"I..." He swallowed hard. "I just thought it was something I should do by myself."

"Really?" She sighed. "That's sad, honey. Sad and lonely and weird." She leaned forward and kissed his other cheek. "We should talk about that later," she told him. "I'm starting to get the feeling that there's a lot going on in your head right now that I don't understand. You haven't been buying any old houses without telling me, have you? I mean, if you want to have a midlife crisis, can't you get a bike or a speedboat like a normal person?"

"It's tiny," Scott said, returning to the hallway after an exploratory trip to the front room, with his sister in tow. "Did you really used to live here, Dad?"

"I did," he replied, forcing a smile. "Back when I was your age."

"Huh." Clearly unimpressed, Scott headed through to the kitchen, and again Katie followed. She was like her brother's shadow, especially when they were away from home. Safety in numbers.

"So you decided to all come and surprise me, huh?" John said, turning back to Sarah.

"Something wrong with that?"

"Not at all."

"I know you probably wanted to have some quiet time alone," she continued, "but when Reginald told me exactly what was going on, with buying this place and all, I just couldn't shake the feeling that it all seemed..." She paused, as if she couldn't find the right word. "Unhealthy," she added finally. "The thought of you being here alone, rattling around with your thoughts, just worried me. I couldn't leave the kids with anyone, so I had to bring them, but anyway I figured they should see where their father came from. Please, tell me you're not mad at me for surprising you."

He stared at he for a moment. "Of course not," he said eventually. "I just... I don't have anything in, that's all. Maybe we should go out and get breakfast in town." As the words left his mouth, he realized that the last thing he wanted was to end up at the cafe where Hannah worked, although... Pausing, he realized he couldn't quite remember Hannah leaving last night, although he was sure she'd left at some point. "Or I could pop to the petrol station and pick something up. Maybe that'd be better."

"Is there a basement?" Scott called through from the kitchen. "There's a hatch in the floor!"

"It's locked," John said quickly.

"So how was last night?" Sarah asked with a smile. "How was the book club with your adoring fans?"

"Fine."

"Were you there late?"

He swallowed hard. "No. I was home before midnight."

"Home?" She paused. "You call this place home?"

"You know what I mean. It was... Nothing much happened."

"And how was it sleeping here last night?"

"Fine," he replied, taking a deep breath. "Uneventful, you know?"

"Lonely?"

"I was fine."

"And what were your little groupies like?" she asked, heading through to the front room and taking a look around. "Did you have lots of adoring fans throwing themselves at you?" She turned to him with a smile. "If some hot young fan tried to seduce you, I hope you managed to control yourself."

"Come on," he replied, "remember who you're talking to here."

"The man who used to be my reserved, publicity-shy husband," she continued, "and who now apparently goes to fan club meetings."

"It wasn't a fan club meeting, it was a book club. It was barely even that, it was just a few people sitting around talking about what they were reading."

"And then a real superstar writer showed up in their midst, huh?"

"It was interesting to hear their thoughts," he replied, as Scott and Katie ran through and then began to bound upstairs. "Hey! Wait!" he called after them.

Stopping, they turned to him. "What's wrong?" Scott asked. "Aren't we allowed to go upstairs?"

"I..." John paused. "Sure you are. Just be careful, that's all."

"Are those your cigarettes in the kitchen?" Katie asked.

"Cigarettes?" He paused. "Um... No. No, those were there when I arrived. I guess the previous owners left them behind."

"You seem nervy," Sarah told him as the kids headed up to the landing. "I mean, you're always kinda nervy, but it's different this time. Being in this place has really got to you, huh?"

"Actually," he replied, "I've been clearing my head."

"Did you drink wine last night?" Scott called down from upstairs. "There's an empty wine bottle in one of the rooms!"

Sarah raised a skeptical but amused eyebrow. "Clearing your head, huh?"

"I just..." He paused, trying to remember exactly when and why he'd bought a bottle of wine, although the events of the previous night were still a little hazy. "I guess I just fancied a drink. Is that so wrong?"

"Oh no," she replied, stepping closer, "there's *nothing* wrong with buying the childhood home where you lived with your crazy grandmother, secretly running off there without telling your loving and very understanding wife, changing aspects of your personality seemingly on a dime, and then drinking a bottle of wine all by yourself. That's normal behavior, John. Everyone does that, it's practically a rite of passage."

"You're reading too much into this," he told her, before spotting the bottle opener and cork on the carpet, close to a splash of spilled wine. Again, he didn't remember any of that, although he had a vague memory of drinking wine straight from the bottle. "There's nothing going on," he continued, forcing a smile. "I'm just surprised to see you, that's all. I was planning to head back to the house later."

"The house?" She stared at him for a moment. "So this place is home, and our place is just the house?"

He sighed. "You know what I meant."

"Well now we're here," she continued, with a smile, "it'll just have to be the summer holiday we hadn't got around to planning yet, won't it? I didn't drive all the way down with the kids just to turn around and go straight back to London, so why don't you show us around your old hometown? You always refused to bring me here before."

"There's not much to show you."

"What about your old haunts? Sorry, bad choice of words, but..." Stepping closer, she put her hands on his shoulders. "You've always been so reserved when it comes to talking about your past, John. Maybe it's time to put that straight. Come on, at least for twenty-four hours, can't you show us where you really come from?"

"I..." Sighing, he realized he had no choice. "Let me just get my jacket."

Heading upstairs, he took a quick look in all the rooms, just to make absolutely certain that Hannah had left. He was still trying to remember exactly what had happened, but he figured the wine had made his memory a little glitchy. There was no sign of her, so obviously she'd left, and he figured he needed to be less paranoid. After all, he had nothing to hide, and the house was just a house. He had nothing to hide.

CHAPTER SIXTEEN

Twenty years ago

"YES, SHE DID," JOHN SAID, shocked by the news of his friend's disappearance. "Just a few days ago, actually. She came and we hung out, and she stayed the night before heading back to Peterborough."

"And that was the last time you saw Alison?" the officer asked, making a note as he sat at the kitchen table.

John nodded.

"And she definitely said she was driving back to Peterborough?"

"She did. I'm sure of it."

"And what time did she leave here?" the other officer, a woman, asked.

"Early," he said, turning to her. She seemed more the more skeptical of the two officers, as if she didn't entirely believe his story. "When it was getting light, whatever time that was. Seven, maybe eight."

"Where was her car parked?"

"I'm not sure. I didn't see it." He paused. "Haven't you found it?"

"About half a mile away," the male officer explained, still making notes. "We've spoken to her parents and they don't know why she'd have parked in Vauxhall Road, but we're still looking into that. You don't happen to know whether she had any friends in that area, do you?"

John shook his head.

"So you're the only person she knows around here?" the female officer asked.

Turning to her, John realized that she definitely seemed the more suspicious of the two of them, as if she actually thought he might be hiding something.

"She just dropped by because she was home for a couple of days," he explained, trying not to let on that he was starting to panic. "She did that about three or four times a year."

"And were you and her..." The female officer paused, as if she wasn't quite sure how to phrase the next question. "Well, I have to ask. Was your relationship with Abigail of a romantic nature?"

He shook his head.

"Just friends, then?"

"Just friends. Totally."

"But she stayed the night?"

"In a separate room."

"Right." The female officer paused again. "And you live here by yourself?"

John nodded.

"Do you own the property?"

"My father does. I lived here with my grandmother, but she passed away a few days ago."

"I'm sorry to hear that," she told him, glancing around the room. "So now it's just you?"

"For now. I'm still working out what to do. I haven't had much time to think, though, because of the funeral and everything."

"How did she die?" the male officer asked, not looking up from his notebook.

"Aneurysm, I think," John replied.

"Quick," he muttered. "At least that's something." He turned to a new page and made some more notes. "My Nan died of one of those. Much better than my Grandad, he had a stroke. Now *that's* no way to go. He was basically like a vegetable for a while, although he seemed kind of aware of everyone around him. He recovered a little, but not much, not enough to really have any kind of a life. At least with an aneurysm, it can be as quick as just keeling over like someone's flicked a switch. Small blessings, eh?"

"I suppose," John replied, before seeing that the female officer was still watching him with a hint of suspicion. "I'm sure you'll find Alison soon. She's only been gone, what, two days?"

"That's still a long time for a young woman to be out of contact with everyone she knows," the female officer pointed out. "No phone calls, no ATM visits, no sightings. Plus, if she hasn't got her car with her... Do you know if she might have anything she wants to keep from her parents? A secret boyfriend, maybe, or something that might cause a problem in her life?"

"She has a boyfriend in Peterborough."

"I'm aware of that, but we're looking for something closer to home. Drug use?"

He shook his head.

"I think we've got everything we came for," the male officer said, closing his notebook and getting to his feet. "Obviously, since so far you're the last person to see her, we might have to come back and ask you some more questions. And if she gets in touch with you in any way, please tell her to contact her parents or to at least give us a call at the station, just so we know she's safe. She's not in any trouble, people are just worried about her."

"Of course," John replied, leading them to the hallway and opening the door. "You don't think anything's actually happened, do you?"

"Nah," the male officer said, "it's probably nothing."

"It could be something," his colleague added, following him out to the front step and then turning to John. "We take it very seriously when young women go missing. There have been some nasty cases in recent years and we don't want Alison Blackstock being added to that list, do we?"

"I'm sure she's fine," John replied, swallowing hard as he realized he was probably coming across as a little weird. Trying to look more relaxed, he forced a smile, although he immediately felt that this hadn't really worked. "Say hi to her when you find her," he added, before realizing that this, too, might seem strange.

Once the two officers were gone, John lingered in the kitchen, keeping just out of sight as he watched them out by the front gate. They hadn't got into their patrol car yet, and instead they were talking while the male officer looked through his notebook. Taking great care not to get spotted, John could tell that whatever they were talking about, it seemed to be causing a minor disagreement between the two of them, and finally he ducked back as the female officer turned and looked toward the house. He waited, worried that they were about to come back with more questions, but thirty seconds later he heard a car door being slammed, following by the sound of an engine starting.

Peering back out through the window, he saw to his relief that the police car was pulling away. Even though he knew he hadn't done anything wrong, he'd felt distinctly uneasy during the officers' visit, but he told himself there was no point worrying now, that he just had to relax. Sighing, he headed across the kitchen, stepping over the hatch to the basement as he made his way to the stairs.

CHAPTER SEVENTEEN

Today

"CHRIST, IT'S WINDY OUT HERE," John said, as a gale blew in across the sea and the beach, "are you sure you don't want to get out of this weather?"

"And miss seeing where you grew up?" Sarah asked, even as her hair was blown across her face. "You've spent the past decade very carefully *not* telling me much about your old life. It's catch-up time." She looked across the beach and saw Scott and Katie throwing pebbles into the rough sea, trying in vain to make them skim the surface. "Besides, the kids are loving it. When was the last time they got to play on a beach, huh?"

"Sure," John muttered, clearly feeling uncomfortable as he adjusted his scarf.

"So was that you once?" she asked, spotting a group of teenagers hanging around a derelict bandstand a little further up ahead. "Did you and your mates sit around, talking and wasting the days? Setting fire to bins, that sort of thing?"

"No," he said with a faint smile, "nothing like that."

"Somehow I figured. I'm guessing you were a good boy, weren't you? Safe and sound at home?"

"Something like that."

"But you had friends, right? I know you don't seem to be in contact with anyone from around here anymore, but you had friends back then, didn't you?"

"Of course."

"Thank God. I was starting to worry you were some kind of loner. So tell me about them."

"Well... I don't know, there were a few people. Mainly from school."

"Are you going to look them up while you're in town?"

He smiled at the suggestion. "No, I don't think so."

"Why not?"

"Because that was all twenty years ago."

"So maybe it'd be fun to catch up," she replied, as they stopped to watch the kids still throwing pebbles. "Twenty years is a long time, a lot can happen. Besides, you've become this rich, successful author. Don't you want to show off a little?"

He shook his head.

"What about a girlfriend?"

He turned to her.

"You must have had a girlfriend around here," she continued with a faint, knowing smile. "Did you come down and snog her on the beach after dark?"

"No snogging."

"Wasn't there anyone?" she asked, seemingly a little disappointed.

"I..." He paused. "I had a few female friends."

"Name one."

"Uh... Well, there was Alison Blackstock."

"Ooh, Alison Blackstock," she said with a grin, as a seagull waddled past. "Sounds like a right little tart. Come on, then, spill the beans, how were things between you and this Alison Blackstock hussy?"

"We were just friends."

"Really? That's kind of disappointing, John. I'd like to think you had at least one bout of teenage kicks while you lived here." She stared at him for a moment, watching as the wind ruffled his hair. "Don't take this the wrong way, but you were really a bit of a shut-in, weren't you?"

"You make me sound like a hermit."

They both turned as they heard shouting from the bandstand. They watched for a moment as a minor scuffle broke about among the teenagers, but whatever had caused the argument was quickly diffused and a couple of hoodie-wearing boys sulked off, leaving the others with their energy drinks.

"You'd rather I'd been like that?" John asked, turning to Sarah. "Seriously?"

"I'd like to think you were doing *something* productive with your time," she continued, still watching the teenagers. "No-one's a saint, John. You need to learn the rules of social interaction from somewhere. I mean, those kids aren't hurting anyone, are they? It's normal for a teenager to want to rebel against. I hate to break this to you, but when our kids become teenagers, we're in for a world of stress." She turned to him. "Didn't you ever want to rebel when you were younger?"

"I was just trying to find my way."

She stared at him for a moment, before leaning closer and planting a kiss on his cheek. "I love you," she told him. "I just wish you'd had a better childhood."

"I can't blame my childhood for everything."

"But still -"

"I was fine. I got by."

She turned and looked at Scott and Katie, who were still throwing pebbles into the sea.

"So are you going to contact her?" she asked finally.

"Who?"

"Alison Blackstock."

He opened his mouth to reply, but at the last moment he held back. "No."

"No? Come on, it might be fun."

"I can't."

"Doesn't she live around here anymore?"

"She..." He paused, watching as Scott managed to get a pebble to skip a few times. "She disappeared, actually," he continued finally, turning to her. "She just upped and vanished one day and no-one ever heard from her again. So no, I don't think I can contact her, because as far as I know she's still missing."

***

"It's just Reginald," he said a little while later, checking his buzzing phone as the four of them sat in a cafe near the beach. He took a moment to read the text message. "Huh. He's got in touch with the couple who owned the house before I bought it back."

"Why's he done that?" Sarah asked, glancing up from the menu.

"Oh, I..." He paused. "I asked him to, that's all, but it doesn't matter now. Turns out they only moved across town, but..." His voice trailed off for a moment, before he put his phone away. "Never mind."

"What did you want to talk to them about?"

"Just their experiences in the house."

"Such as?"

"Such as..." He paused again, wishing that he'd never mentioned the message at all. "Honey, I'm a writer, I look for stories wherever I think I can find them. I had this vague idea that I wanted to know what life had been like for them in that house, but suddenly it doesn't seem quite so interesting."

"Huh." She watched as he studied the menu. "Seems a bit odd, that's all," she continued finally. "I mean, you obviously cared enough to get Reginald to contact them, and now suddenly you're not interested. Is there something about the house that you're not telling us?"

"Like what?" he asked, trying to sound casual.

"It's not..." She paused. "It's not, like, haunted or something, is it?"

He turned to her.

She smiled.

"John, it's not, is it?"

"Of course it's not. No house is haunted."

"Is the house haunted?" Scott asked. "Really?"

"No!" John said firmly.

"Wow," Katie said, her eyes wide with shock.

"Nothing's haunted," John continued, trying not to sound annoyed. "There's no such things as ghosts."

"Says a man who writes about ghosts."

"That doesn't mean I believe in them," he replied, clearly a little irritated as he tried to focus on the menu. "Does everyone know what they want?"

"I want to see a ghost," Scott told him.

"Well, you can't. You'd have better luck trying to see a unicorn."

"But unicorns aren't real," Katie said. "*Are* they?"

"We have to order at the counter," John said, getting to his feet. "Scott, I take it you want a burger? And Katie, I take it you want whatever Scott's having?" They both nodded, and he turned to his wife. "Honey?"

"Burger too, thanks," she replied, and then she watched as he headed to the counter.

"Is Dad mad at us?" Scott asked after a moment.

"No, sweetie," she replied, turning to him with a smile, "your father's just... on edge."

"Why?"

"I'm not entirely sure."

"So is the house really haunted?"

"Is it?" Katie asked, leaning past her brother. "Is it really, Mum?"

"Of course not," Sarah replied, setting the laminated menus back in the holder. "Your father's right, there's no such thing as ghosts." She watched as John placed their order at the counter, and for a moment she felt a shiver of concern pass through her chest. "There's nothing to worry about," she added. "After all, it's just a house."

CHAPTER EIGHTEEN

Twenty years ago

"I JUST WASN'T EXPECTING YOU," John said, feeling a sense of panic in his gut as he watched his father walking across the kitchen. "You didn't call to say you were coming. You usually call."

After looking out at the street for a moment, Graham turned to his son. "I just thought I'd surprise you," he said with a smile. "See how you're keeping up without giving you a chance to put on a show." He paused for a moment. "How *are* you keeping up, anyway? It's been a month since your gran died. Sorry I couldn't fly over sooner."

"Everything's fine."

"Fine?"

John nodded.

"Just fine?" Graham asked.

"What else should it be?"

Graham looked around the kitchen for a moment, as if he expected to see something of interest. "And you've just spent the past month pottering about the house?"

"I've been tidying."

"How was the funeral?"

"Fine."

"Sorry I didn't get to it. Did many people show up?"

"Loads. Mainly old people, I had to shake a lot of hands."

"And you had no trouble organizing it?"

"It was pretty easy," he explained. "I just went down to the funeral parlor near the train crossing and they basically took over from there. I used the money you sent me last year for tuition fees."

"You did, did you?" Graham paused, staring at him with a hint of suspicion. "Well, I guess I'll have to send you some more to cover *actual* tuition fees, won't I? When you finally get around to deciding which university you want to go to, at least." He made his way over to the breakfast bar and then looked down at the hatch to the basement for a moment, before heading to the door that led into the hallway and giving the wall a quick knock, as if to check that it was still solid. "Of course, we'll have to sell this place."

"Why?"

"You're gonna move away to university, aren't you?"

"I... suppose so..."

"Then there's no point hanging onto the house. I was thinking I could sell it and buy somewhere in the town where you decide to move to. Then you can take a room and I can rent out the others to a couple of other lads from your course." He turned to John and smiled. "You'll have housemates. How does that sound?"

"Um..." John paused, feeling genuinely horrified by the thought living with other people. "Fine."

"There's that word again," Graham continued, heading back across the room and putting his hands on his son's shoulders, as if he was getting ready to shake him. "Fine. Is everything merely *fine*, my boy? Don't you ever think life could be *better* than fine?"

"I..." John frowned. "Yeah, I guess."

Graham stared at him for a moment longer, before starting to laugh. "Oh boy," he chucked, "you lived such a sheltered life here with your gran, didn't you? When you get out there into the real world, you're really gonna have to adjust so there's -"

Stopping suddenly, he looked up at the

ceiling.

"What was that?" he asked after a moment.

John looked up too. "What was what?"

Graham paused, before turning back to him. "Nothing. Probably just old Lizzie's ghost, pissed off that I've set foot in the place." He put an arm around John's shoulder and began to lead him to the hallway. "Now let's take a look around the place. You and me, son, we've got some catching-up to do. In fact, why don't we start by getting out of here for the evening? When was the last time you had a proper night on the town?"

"Um..."

***

"What about *her*?" Graham asked, leaning past John for a moment to get a better view of the girl at the corner table. "She looks like she's about your age. A little slutty maybe, but that's alright, you're not looking for someone to marry."

Smiling awkwardly, John looked down at the beer his father had placed in front of him, and which he knew he'd have to drink at some point. Between that and the foul cigarette smoke filling the pub, he felt genuinely nauseous.

"Or her," Graham continued. "Jesus, look at the legs on that one. You wanna go and get her phone number soon, or I might just beat you to it.

All's fair in love and war."

"I'm fine," John replied, before realizing that he'd used that word again.

"You're not fine," Graham told him. "You've spent far too long knocking about that house with your grandmother. Lizzie might not have been a bad woman in some respects, but she had a very funny way of looking at the world and some of it has definitely rubbed off on you. I'm worried she made you too insular, too prone to sitting alone and just thinking about things. The world's for living, John, not for watching on TV. I mean, look at some of the women on display in this place, don't you want to take one of them home some time and have a good time?"

"I write," John muttered.

"Yeah, well..." Rolling his eyes, Graham took a sip of beer. "No offense, but I think you're gonna need a bit more on your side than a few short stories. What kind of stuff do you write, anyway?"

"This and that. Science-fiction, horror..."

"Well that's not gonna get you anywhere," Graham continued. "Again, no offense, but I'm worried your grandmother has made you turn a little weird."

"Weird?"

"You're folding in on yourself, boy. I could see it as soon as I arrived this morning, you're disappearing. I know it's not going to be an easy job, getting you out of your shell, it takes time to undo the kind of damage Liz did to you." He paused for a moment, watching John with a hint of caution. "I probably shouldn't say this," he continued finally, "and I know it's gonna sound a little mean, but in some ways I'm actually relieved that she's gone. Not that I wish death on anyone, but you have to understand that your grandmother was a very bad influence on you."

John lifted the beer to his lips and took a sip. It tasted like bread.

"Liz was a complicated woman," Graham muttered, taking another glug of beer. "She never liked me, for a start. Thought I was too rough for her daughter, although she came round a little when she realized I had money. But she always looked down on me, especially after your mother died. She blamed me, which was rubbish. If you ask me, your grandmother did a number on your mother long before I ever arrived on the scene. She got into her head and never really let go, she twisted her thoughts and I'm worried she did the same thing to you." He waited for a reply. "One thing that is not going to happen, my boy, is that you are not going to sit around in that house."

"I was thinking -"

"I'm selling it," Graham added. "Definitely. I'll go down the estate agent's office tomorrow."

"But -"

"No buts, it's decided." He clinked his glass against John's. "Don't worry, I'll still support you. I believe in you, I know you can turn out alright once you're free from your grandmother's shadow." He paused for a moment. "She never hit you, did she? Or... touched you?"

"What do you mean?" John asked.

"Your mother used to say things," he continued. "I never really knew if they were true, but she said your grandmother had a bit of a temper, and that she used to fly into these rages. Your mother had a few scars that she said were from your grandmother. I kind of dismissed it all at the time, but... That never happened with you, did it?"

John paused, before shaking his head.

"That time I came to visit," Graham added, "and you had a big bruise on the side of your face... You really *did* fall down the stairs, didn't you?"

John nodded.

"Huh." Pausing, Graham stared at him for a moment longer. "Well, whatever, the past is in the past and today is a new day. Or night, whatever." He looked over at a girl sitting alone at the next table. "So are you gonna ask for her number, or do I have to do it for you?"

"Dad, please..."

"Oi!" Graham called out, leaning toward the girl. "You alright on your own there? You wanna come and sit with us for a bit?"

Looking faintly disgusted by the offer, the girl turned away from them.

"Suit yourself," Graham muttered, turning to John with a smile. "You never know until you try, do you? Don't worry, they won't all be as stuck-up as her, some of 'em like the direct approach. Believe it or not, John, one day you'll meet a nice girl. And when that happens, you'll barely even remember this crumby little town." He raised his half-empty glass for a toast. "To leaving this place and never looking back."

John raised his glass, even though he felt distinctly uncomfortable.

"And to a new life far from here," Graham continued. "I promise, when you finally leave, you'll never want to even think about this town or your old life again, and that's exactly how it should be. Take my advice, son. Once you leave a place, never go back."

CHAPTER NINETEEN

Today

"MUM," A VOICE WHISPERED IN THE DARKNESS, as a hand nudged her shoulder. "Mum, wake up."

Opening her eyes, Sarah saw Scott silhouetted against the window.

"What's wrong?" she asked, sitting up in bed.

"We're scared."

Looking past Scott for a moment, Sarah saw that Katie was standing a little further back. Turning, she grabbed her phone and checked the time, finding that it was a little after 3am.

"Why are you scared?" she asked, turning back to the children. "There's no reason to be scared."

"We heard noises," Katie whispered.

"What kind of noises?"

"In the house," Scott said, with tension in his voice.

Turning, Sarah saw that John was sleeping soundly next to her.

"Did you lie to us earlier?" Scott asked. "Is the house haunted after all?"

"No, sweetie," she said, pulling the duvet aside and swinging her legs down onto the carpet. "What kind of noises did you hear, exactly?"

"There was someone in the kitchen," Scott said matter-of-factly.

"Uh-huh," Katie added, nodding solemnly.

"I'm sure -"

"We went and checked," Scott added, "but we couldn't see anyone. We still heard them, though."

"You went and checked?"

He nodded. "Katie wanted to wake you up right away, but I told her we should look first, in case it was nothing."

"Well, that was very brave of you," she replied, getting to her feet and heading to the door, "but you should have come to wake us up first." She leaned out into the dark hallway and saw that a light was on down in the kitchen. "Did you two turn that on?" she asked.

"To make Katie less scared," Scott whispered, standing just behind her.

"You're the one who wanted it on," Katie told him.

"So what exactly do you think you heard?" Sarah asked.

"I heard someone banging," Katie continued.

"I heard a voice," Scott added. "It was really muffled, though. It sounded like someone whispering. It didn't last long, but... It sounded like whoever it was, they were in pain."

"Well, that..." Sarah paused for a moment. "I guess your father and I really freaked you out earlier, didn't we, talking about ghosts and stuff?" She reached down and took their hands. "Come on, let's go take a quick look and make sure there's nothing whispering down there."

"Shouldn't we wake Dad?" Scott asked.

"Let him sleep," she replied, leading them through the door and then down the stairs. "He had trouble nodding off earlier, so let's just take a quick look down here and then we can go back to bed, okay?" Reaching the door to the kitchen, she found the harsh electric light a little overpowering. "See? There's no-one here."

"There was a voice earlier," Scott said, clearly very skeptical.

"We're not making it up," Katie added.

"I know you're not," Sarah replied, letting go of their hands and checking to make sure the door was locked, "but if -"

Suddenly there was a faint bump from nearby. She turned and looked across the kitchen, but there was no sign of anything. A moment later, she felt the children grabbing her hands again.

"Mum," Katie whispered, "I think it came from the basement."

***

"Of course there's no light switch," Sarah muttered, fumbling in the darkness at the top of the stairs that led down into the pitch-black basement. "Why would there be a light switch? That'd just be too convenient, wouldn't it?"

"Do you see anything?" Katie asked, holding the hatch open.

Staring down into the basement, Sarah squinted but still couldn't make anything out.

"Here," Scott said suddenly, reaching through with her mobile phone. "I tried waking Dad, but he was snoring."

"Thanks." Bringing up the flashlight app, Sarah held the phone out and saw that the rickety wooden stairs led down to a concrete floor below. The walls looked to be made of breeze-blocks, rough and dusty. "You two stay up here, okay? I'm just going to go down and take a look to make sure there's nothing to worry about."

"What if there's something down there?" Katie asked.

"The house was just sold. There'll be nothing down here at all." She paused for a moment, feeling a little nervous, before keeping her head low as she made her way carefully down the creaking steps. With the phone still held out, she could see a wall of breeze blocks to one side, but to her surprise she realized that there were cobwebs hanging from the ceiling and various old, damp cardboard boxes near the foot of the stairs, as if the previous owners hadn't cleaned the place out when they left.

"Do you see anything?" Scott called out from the hatch.

"Not yet, sweetie," she replied, reaching the bottom of the stairs and shining the phone around.

The basement was much smaller than she'd imagined, and there was a distinctly bitter smell in the cold air. Taking a few steps forward, she saw that the place was a mess, with rotten boxes everywhere and old jars that in some cases had broken and leaked thick black liquid all over the floor. When she leaned down and lifted the lid on one of the boxes, she found a bunch of old books inside. Scrunching her nose up slightly, she took care not to set her bare feet on anything too gross as she made her way to the far wall, which at least seemed to have less grime caked all over its surface. She waited, but there was no hint of a sound and as she turned and looked around once again, she told herself that the bump must just have been the house settling, although she wasn't entirely sure whether that was something that really happened to houses or whether it was just something people talked about in movies.

"Cool!" Scott said suddenly, having made his way down the stairs with his sister right behind.

"Hey!" Sarah hissed, reaching out and grabbing his shoulder. "Careful! There's all sorts of stuff down here, I have no idea whether it's safe."

"This place stinks," Scott pointed out, turning to Katie. "Don't you think so?"

She nodded.

"Whatever," Sarah continued, "there's clearly nothing down here, okay guys? How about we go back up and get some sleep? I'm kind of cold."

"Can we sleep down here?" Scott asked. "It'd be like camping."

"No way. Get back up to the kitchen."

"But -"

"Now!"

As the children headed back up the stairs, Sarah took one last look around the basement, and she couldn't help but wonder why the previous owners had left so much junk behind. The rest of the house seemed so clean and well-maintained, whereas the basement seemed not to have been touched for years. Heading to the foot of the stairs, she began to make her way up, and then finally she and the children closed the hatch, leaving the basement in darkness again.

After a moment, there was another faint bump, this time too quiet to be heard in the rest of the house.

CHAPTER TWENTY

Twenty years ago

"JESUS CHRIST," GRAHAM MUTTERED, swaying as he stood in the kitchen, "I'm actually drunk." He squinted as he tried to look at his watch. "What time is it? Three? Does that say three?"

"Ten to three," John told him as he locked the front door. "It's late. I think I'm going to bed."

"What about your gran's port stash?" Graham asked. "Please tell me you didn't pour it all down the sink."

"Sorry."

"Bloody hell," Graham muttered, looking around the kitchen, "so the whole house is dry, eh?"

"Sorry."

"Stop apologizing. I should've known.

Should've picked up some beer from the corner shop. Maybe even something stronger. I can't believe that stupid club shut at two. What the hell is wrong with this town?"

"There might be an old bottle of sherry in the cabinet," John told him.

"Then fetch it, my boy!" Graham roared, his cheeks rosy red with enthusiasm. "Go! Go! Bring me that sherry, and two glasses to go with it! You'll have some, even if I have to pour it down your throat myself!"

Smiling awkwardly, and already wondering why he'd even mentioned the sherry, John turned and headed to the front room. He could hear his father bumping about in the kitchen, and as he opened the cabinet door and reached inside, he felt the bottle of sherry at the back. Pulling it out, he saw to his relief that at least it was half empty, so he grabbed two glasses and made his way back to the kitchen.

"I really don't think I like this stuff," he explained. "I never got why -"

Stopping suddenly in the doorway, he looked around the kitchen and saw no sign of his father. A moment later, with a sudden sense of horror, he realized that the hatch leading down to the basement had been opened, and he could hear his father drunkenly stumbling about down there.

"No!" John called out, setting the bottle and

glasses on the counter before rushing to the hatch and making his way down into the dark basement below, where he almost collided with his father in the darkness.

"What the bloody hell's going on down here?" Graham asked, his beer-soaked breath filling the damp air as he pushed past John and made his way toward the far end of the basement. "Was this place always so small?"

"What do you mean?" John asked, feeling a sense of panic that he couldn't quite explain. He'd mostly stayed out of the basement since his grandmother had died, and now he was filled with a surprisingly strong level of fear. Taking his phone from his pocket, he used the screen to bring a little light to the room.

"Is this wall new?" Graham continued, running his hands over the breeze-blocks. "I swear it wasn't like this when I bought the house."

"I think it's always been there," John told him. "Nothing's changed. Why would it have changed?"

"Doesn't make any bloody sense," Graham muttered, stumbling drunkenly to the other end of the wall. "This definitely seems new. I can smell the cement still." He leaned closer to the wall to give it a sniff, only to bump his nose against the rough surface. "I know a freshly-laid wall when I find one," he muttered. "There definitely used to be more to this basement. Someone's put this wall up in the past day or two."

"I think she had some work done a few months ago," John replied, still not sure why he felt so panic-stricken. All he could think about was that he had to get his father out of the basement as fast as possible, but when he grabbed his father's arm and tried to lead him back to the stairs, he realized physical force wouldn't be enough. "I don't remember exactly what it was about, but there was definitely a builder down here for a few days."

"She didn't mention it to me," Graham grumbled, crouching in the corner and bumping his fist against one of the breeze-blocks, which turned out to be slightly loose. "She was supposed to let me know about any work she had done on the house. After all, I'm the one who owns the damn place." He sighed. "Then again, the old cow wasn't exactly keen to give me a call, was she?" He bumped the loose breeze-block again. "Whoever she got in to do this, it definitely wasn't anyone who knew what they were doing. Some of these aren't in place properly."

"I don't know who did it," John said, "but I think -"

"Bloody hell!" Graham said suddenly, pulling back slightly. "Did you hear that?"

"Hear what?"

Graham paused. "Must be rats. Christ, what

kind of job has she had done down here? She's obviously hired some complete amateur. Hell, aren't these the breeze-blocks that were out in the garden, behind the greenhouse? Why's she sectioned off half the effin' basement? Mad old bat."

"I think there was a leak," John replied.

Graham turned to him. "So she just sealed it off?"

"She got it fixed and then... Yeah, she got it sealed off."

"A leak of what? All the pipes are on this side."

"I don't know," John replied, "but why don't we go up and try the sherry? I found the bottle and -"

"Can't have rats running free," Graham continued, turning and pressing his ear against the wall. "I can hear the buggers scurrying about in there. Christ, if they get settled, they could overrun the whole bloody house, not to mention chewing through the wiring. I bought this place as an investment, but rats are gonna really scupper my plans." Muttering something else under his breath, he started tugging on the loose block. "Let's get to those rats, eh? Bring the sherry bottle down here, boy, and I'll show you how to kill a rat with your bare hands."

"Dad -"

"Go on. Get the bottle."

"Dad..."

"What?" With the breeze-block already partway out of the wall, he turned to John in the darkness. "Why are you -"

Before he could finish, John brought a metal pole crashing down against the top of his father's head.

***

"Oh..." Graham muttered, opening his eyes slowly and finding himself sprawled across the sofa in the front room, with morning light streaming through the window. "What..."

He began to sit up, before feeling a splitting pain in his head. Letting out a faint gasp, he reached up and felt dried blood in his scalp, and a moment later he realized his gut was churning. He was hungover, that much was certain, but as he continued to run his fingers through his hair he felt a shallow cut that had already begun to heal.

"What the bloody hell..."

"Hey."

Turning, Graham saw John sitting nearby in one of the armchairs with a faint smile.

"What happened?" Graham asked, looking around the room with a frown.

"Are you okay?" John replied. "I almost called an ambulance, but then you started snoring so

I just dragged you through here and figured you needed to sleep it off."

"Sleep what off?" Graham muttered, wincing at the pain in his head. "How much did I drink last night, exactly?"

"Don't you remember?"

Graham paused, before shaking his head. "I remember going to that pub, and we had a few beers, then we went to that rubbish little club and then we came back here and..." He paused again, waiting for a few more memories to surface through the fog that was filling his thoughts. "It gets a bit hazy after that," he added, before spotting the empty bottle of sherry nearby on the carpet. "Did we drink that?"

"*You* did," John told him. "I had a sip, but I didn't really like it. You drank half a bottle."

"Oh Christ," Graham continued, putting his head in his hands for a moment. "I don't even like the damn stuff most of the time."

"And then you fell down the stairs," John added.

Graham turned to him. "I *what*?"

"Only from halfway. You were heading up to the bathroom, and then I heard you cry out, and then there was a loud bump and I found you at the bottom. I think you hit your head on the corner of the table in the hallway. There was some blood but, like I said, it didn't seem too bad. You were pretty lucky."

"I don't remember any of that," Graham
muttered, struggling to his feet and swaying
slightly. "Still, my stomach feels like..." He paused,
as if he was on the verge of throwing up. "It's been
a while since I've managed to get quite so wasted.
You might not be much of a drinker, John, but
you're a hell of a wing-man when it comes to these
things." He frowned. "It feels like my stomach is
upside down."

"So you really don't remember anything
from after we got back to the house last night?"
John asked.

Graham shook his head.

"Nothing at all?"

"I always get blackouts when I mix drinks,"
Graham muttered, stumbling toward the door.
Checking his watch, he sighed. "Christ, I have to
leave for the airport in a few hours."

"That's a shame," John replied calmly. "You
won't have time to do very much at all, will you?"

"I need to shower," Graham replied,
stopping for a moment, "and I need to..." He
paused, before wincing slightly. "Oh God, I think
I'm gonna hurl!"

John sat and listened as his father raced
upstairs, and then he heard the sound of loud,
painful vomiting in the bathroom. Although he
knew he should go and ask if there was anything he

could do to help, he could only think about the fact that he'd managed to get his father out of the basement. He couldn't remember why he'd been so worried about the wall down there, and he felt as if his thoughts didn't quite make sense, but he figured he could work that out later. For now, he felt calm again, as if everything was back to normal.

Upstairs, his father was still throwing up after all the sherry that had literally been poured down his throat the night before.

CHAPTER TWENTY-ONE

Today

"WHO'S HANNAH?"

Looking up from his laptop, John saw that Sarah was standing in the doorway.

"John," she continued, with a worried expression, "two guys are here, they want to talk to you. They say some girl named Hannah is missing, and they think maybe you're the last person who saw her."

***

"Hang on," Gary said, interrupting Louis, "let's just stick to the facts. The last time either of us saw Hannah is when she left the flat the other night, to go and talk to you some more, Mr.Myers. We haven't heard from her since."

"Wait a moment," Sarah said, as they all sat in the kitchen, "rewind slightly. Who's this Hannah girl, exactly?"

"Gary's friend," Louis replied.

"No," Gary said, turning to him, "she's *your* friend."

"You're the one who brought her to the flat the first time, a few weeks ago."

"No, you did."

"Dude," Louis continued, "I'd never met her before!"

"Neither had I!"

"Then -"

"Hold up," Sarah said firmly, interrupting them both. "You can argue about the details later, that's not the most important thing right now." She turned to John, and it was clear she was worried. "Did this Hannah girl follow you home the other night?"

"I..." He paused, before taking a deep breath. "Yes, she did. I got back and suddenly she was right behind me."

"She took my wine," Gary added. "And my corkscrew."

"So that empty bottle was hers?" Sarah asked. "John?"

"She said she wanted to talk about my

books," he replied cautiously. "It was late, the last thing I wanted was to talk to anyone about anything, but -"

"So you invited her in?"

"She invited herself in," he continued. "She more or less barged inside."

"More or less?"

"She didn't seem like the kind of girl who takes no for an answer." Sighing, he turned to Gary and Louis. "You guys know what I mean, right?"

They nodded.

"So she wanted to talk about my books," John explained, turning back to his wife and seeing the look of confused concern in her eyes, "and then she wanted to talk about ghosts and haunted houses, and she kind of just went on and on. I mean, the girl could talk for England, really she could. If talking was an Olympic sport, she'd be a gold medallist."

"While drinking wine," Sarah added.

"Yes," he admitted a little reluctantly, "while drinking wine."

"So you were alone here in the house with some teenaged girl," Sarah continued, "drinking wine all night?" She paused. "And you didn't mention this to me until now?"

"I know it sounds bad..."

"Kind of, honey. Kind of."

"It wasn't like that, and she's not a teen. She's early twenties, something like that. I checked."

"Oh, you did?" She raised a skeptical eyebrow. "And why did you do that?"

"It was a completely innocent encounter." He sighed. "She wanted to hang around and see if there was a ghost here, and I couldn't exactly talk her out of it, so I decided to humor her."

"Go on," Sarah said darkly.

"We sat in the room and waited."

"Which room?"

"The room where I found my grandmother."

"Which room is that?"

He sighed again. "The room the kids slept in last night. There was nothing there, nothing happened. No ghost, no nothing, until..." He paused.

"Until what?" Sarah asked.

"There was a noise later on," he continued. "It sounded like something was downstairs, I told her it wasn't anything to worry about but she seemed convinced we were on the verge of seeing a ghost so she came down to look and I followed her."

"And did you see anything?" Gary asked.

"Just an empty kitchen. Anyway, the noise actually seemed to be coming from -" He stopped suddenly, before looking over at the hatch that led down to the basement.

"It came from down there?" Sarah asked.

He nodded.

"So did you go and look?"

"We..." He paused, before offering a faint, cautious smile. "I told her it was locked and that I didn't have a key."

"Which isn't true," Sarah pointed out.

"I just wanted to get rid of her by that point," he continued. "I was tired, it was late, and I didn't exactly fancy spending the rest of the night on some amateur ghost-busting mission. I told her we couldn't go down there, and fortunately she accepted that." He waited for another question. "And then she left," he added finally. "We didn't go into the basement. I swear."

"She left?" Sarah replied. "Just like that?"

"Just like that."

"And that was the last you saw of her?"

He nodded, even though he wasn't entirely sure it was true.

"She's missing," Gary said. "She didn't come back to the flat the next day, and no-one's seen her since."

"Have you contacted her parents?" Sarah asked.

He shrugged. "We don't really know anything about her. She left some stuff at my place, though. Like, some food and a bag, so I think she was planning to come back."

"Have you been to the police?"

"Isn't this an over-reaction?" John asked.

"Do you even know this Hannah girl's surname?"

Gary and Louis looked at each other, and it was clear that neither of them had an answer.

"So she was some kind of drifter," John continued. "I just assumed you guys were friends with her, she seemed to know you pretty well. I mean, she was in your apartment!"

"She was just, like, outgoing," Louis replied.

"She talked her way in a few weeks ago," Gary added. "We don't get many girls doing that. Usually *we're* the ones who have to persuade *them* to come inside."

"You barely knew this girl," John pointed out, "and you don't know a damn thing about her, so it seems to me that she isn't really missing at all. She's just moved on, and if she left some stuff at your place, that doesn't seem particularly unusual. I'm sorry, she didn't say anything to me that might help, she just said goodbye and walked out the door. It never occurred to me that she wasn't going straight back to your place."

"If she's missing," Sarah replied, "we have to do something."

"She's not missing," John said firmly.

"Then where is she?"

"So you want to go to the police?" he asked. "Seriously? And say what, that a girl whose name you don't even know didn't go back to the flat of two guys she'd barely even met? I'm pretty sure

206

they've got more important things to investigate than something like that."

"It just seems off," Gary continued. "Something about this doesn't feel right, it's like..." He paused. "Well, no offense Mr. Myers, but it's almost like the plot of one of your books."

"I don't think I've ever written a book about a girl going missing."

"No, but... I mean, the whole haunted house element."

"There's no haunted house element," John replied with a sigh, getting to his feet and heading to the door. "Look, for all I know, this is some kind of prank. What happened, did you think it'd be funny to try to conjure up some kind of real-life mystery involving a guy like me? Is it all some kind of sick attempt to get attention or notoriety? I wouldn't be surprised if Hannah's in on the whole thing, she's probably waiting around the corner so you can all go and laugh your asses off at my expense." He turned to Sarah. "This is exactly why I don't usually do public appearances. I should never have changed that policy."

"We just want to make sure she's okay," Gary said. "I swear, that's all."

"Have you tried calling her?" Sarah asked.

"We don't have her number."

"Have you tried emailing? Is she on any social networks?"

"We.." Gary paused. "We don't really know. Like I said, we'd barely met her."

"I met her at that cafe on the corner," John said, opening the door and stepping back, as if he was inviting them to leave. "The one by the pier. I don't know how long she'd been working there, maybe it's no help, but it's the only thing I can think to tell you. Now, if you're really worried then I suggest that you go to the police and let them take it from there, but I'm pretty damn sure your so-called friend is long gone by now. I'm sorry, but there's nothing else I can do for you." He paused, waiting for them to take the hint and leave. "Fun time is over," he added finally. "Please. I'm not interested in whatever game you're playing."

***

"So," Sarah said with a faint, cautious smile as John pushed the door shut a few minutes later, "what was all that about, huh?"

"Honey -"

"It's a good job I trust you so much," she continued, stepping closer and putting her hands on his shoulders. "Not many wives would be so happy about their husbands bringing random girls home late at night, drinking wine with them, and then sitting around waiting for ghosts. As stories go, it's not one of your better ones."

"Sarah -"

"But I *do* trust you," she added. "I know you're not that kind of guy. I trust you implicitly, and I know you're more than capable of bumbling your way into a mess like this." She leaned closer and kissed the side of his face. "I just hope this doesn't become a thing."

"A thing?"

"I'm sure she'll turn up," she continued. "It doesn't sound like she really knew those guys anyway. I bet you're right, she's probably some kind of flighty girl who moves on and doesn't think about the people she leaves behind. Still..." She paused for a moment. "You should be careful who you spend time with. She could have been dangerous. She could have been some kind of drug addict."

"She wasn't," he replied. "I could tell."

"The kids thought they heard a noise from the basement last night," she told him. "We took a look, it's filthy down there, but I'm pretty sure I'd have noticed if there had been a girl named Hannah down there."

"You went into the basement?" he asked, clearly alarmed.

"Have you seen the mess the previous occupants left? You should send them the bill to get it cleaned out."

"I'll do it myself," he replied, taking a step back. "Don't go down there again. It might not be safe."

"But honey -"

"I'll clean it up," he continued, "but you're right, it's dirty, God knows what's down there. Promise me that you and the kids won't go down again. I think there are rats, too. They might bite."

"Fine, I promise."

"I'll get started right now," he said, heading to the sink and starting to fill a bucket with water. "Why don't you take the kids out to the beach again? I know we were going to stay until tomorrow, but maybe we should head off tonight? I don't know if I really fancy spending any more time here."

"And what are you going to do with the place once we've left? Rent it out?"

"Maybe. Maybe not."

"You can't just leave it empty."

"Can't I?"

"John -"

"Can you just take the kids out?" he snapped, turning to her. "Please, Sarah, I..." His voice trailed off for a moment, before he sighed and headed back over to her. "Please. I'm sorry, this place is just getting to me, that's all."

"There's a carnival on the seafront tonight," she told him. "I promised the kids we could go."

"But -"

"And then we'll leave first thing in the

morning, okay? I can tell it's not good for you to be here, so we'll leave tomorrow and then we don't ever have to come back." She waited for him to agree. "Please? Like a normal family?"

"Fine," he muttered. "Just one more night."

"But before we leave," she continued, "there's one other thing I think we should do, something that'd be cathartic for you." She paused. "I want you to take me to visit your mother's grave. And your grandmother's. I want to see them."

He opened his mouth to reply, before sighing. "Maybe. If we have time. Right now, my priority is cleaning out that basement."

She watched as he headed to the hatch. Once he'd gone down below, she turned to go and find the children, before spotting her husband's phone resting on the counter-top. She told herself it would be wrong to go through his messages, so she resisted that particular temptation, but as she headed into the dining room she took out her own phone and brought up Reginald's number.

"Hey," she said as soon as he answered, "it's me. I need you to do me a huge favor, and I need you to not mention it to John."

CHAPTER TWENTY-TWO

Twenty years ago

"I THINK IT'LL SELL PRETTY WELL," Graham said as he sipped from his double espresso at the airport bar. "It's a decent house, I'm sure some family's gonna want to take it on."

"Are you sure you have to sell it?" John asked.

"What's wrong, getting sentimental?" Popping two paracetamol out of a packet, Graham dropped them into his mouth and washed them down with more coffee. "That house is no good for you, son. You spent far too long living there with your gran, I should've stepped in a long time ago and done something about it. Still, better late than never, and the old bird's in a better place now." He smiled. "Unless she got taken below."

"Taken below?"

"You know, down to the big red bloke with the horns and the flames."

John nodded, feeling slightly relieved for some reason he didn't quite understand. All day, he'd been feeling as if he'd forgotten something important, and now the sensation seemed more powerful than ever. The events of the previous night with his father were hazy, even hazier than they'd been just a few hours earlier, and he couldn't shake the worry that something was missing from his mind.

"There it is again," Graham said with a faint smile.

John turned to him.

"That vacant expression. I've seen it a couple of times during this visit, it's like your brain switches off for a few seconds and you sorta of... I dunno, you reboot. Are you sure you're feeling okay?"

John nodded.

"I could pay for you to see a shrink if you like."

"No, I'm fine."

"Don't underestimate the damage Liz did to you," Graham continued, before looking around to make sure that no-one could overhear him. "Maybe I shouldn't say this, or maybe I should've said it a long time ago, but your mother told me some pretty dark things about old Elizabeth. She said your grandmother used to scream and yell at her, and call her names, but that wasn't the whole of it. There were marks on your mother's body, old marks, lots of little scars. She had plenty of explanations for them, but none of it ever rang true." He paused, watching John's face for some hint of recognition. "I never said any of this to your mother, of course, but I realized a long time ago that your gran abused her emotionally and psychologically. Physically, too. Your mother once told me she felt like she was being torn in two directions, like the only way to survive was to become two people. How she managed to hold herself together and come out relatively normal is a mystery, but..." He paused again. "Your grandmother was evil. There, I said it." He took another swig of coffee.

"That's a little strong," John replied.

"It's true, though." He took another sip. "I don't have to mince my words on the subject, not anymore. The irony is, she blamed everyone else for your mother's suicide, but if you ask me..." He paused. "Well, maybe that conversation is for another day. Elizabeth was an evil old crone and that house became an extension of her. Even over the past couple of days, I swear I could feel her presence sometimes."

"Like a ghost?" John asked, shocked by the

suggestion.

"Nah, ghosts aren't real," Graham replied. "I heard a few creaks now and then, but that's just how houses are, especially old ones. It was more like... I guess when someone spends a lot of time in one place, and when they have a strong personality, a bit of them gets left behind even after they're dead. That's another reason why you shouldn't spend too much longer in the house. It's unhealthy. Plus, like it or not, I own the damn place and I've made my mind up. I'm selling it." He checked his watch, before finishing his coffee and getting to his feet. "And now, if you'll excuse me, I need to think about going through to the lounge."

"I guess people will want to come and look around," John muttered.

"So keep it tidy," Graham reminded him as they headed toward the security queue. "Don't clutter the place up and..." Stopping at the rear of the queue, he turned to John. "The basement," he said with a frown.

"What about it?" John asked.

"Did we..." He paused. "Did we go down there last night after we got back from the pub?"

"No. Definitely not."

"Are you sure? I've got this vague memory of going down and finding there was an extra wall."

"There's no extra wall," John replied. "We got back, you drank the rest of the sherry, and then you fell down the stairs. That's about it. If you'd opened the hatch to the basement, I'd have known about it."

"Huh. Must've been a dream then." He rolled his eyes. "It's crazy what pops into your head when you're drunk, isn't it?"

"I wouldn't know," John muttered. "You don't have to worry about the basement, though. There's nothing down there." Even as he said those words, however, he felt as if maybe they weren't quite true.

***

"Hello?"

Standing at the top of the steps that led down into the basement, John listened for a moment. He'd been about to go to bed, several hours after getting back from waving his father off, when he'd heard a faint scratching sound from beneath the kitchen. He was reluctant to go down and look, since the basement light hadn't worked for several years, but at the same time he felt drawn to investigate. Something about the basement was bothering him, as if there was something down there that he'd forgotten.

He waited.

Silence.

"Hello?" he called out again.

No reply.

After making his way cautiously down the steps, he headed to the breeze-block wall. His father was right, it definitely hadn't been there before, but at the same time he knew there was no way a wall could just appear out of nowhere. He ran his hands across the surface, and finally he felt some deep, hidden memory starting to float to the surface, as if it had broken free from all the other forgotten memories at the bottom of his mind. He waited, convinced that he was about to understand what he'd forgotten.

For a fraction of a second, he remembered setting one breeze-block on top of two others, and using some kind of paste to seal them together.

As quickly as that memory arrived, however, it was gone again. He knew it had to be false, that there was no way he'd built a wall; after all, he was notoriously unpractical and the idea of him managing to finish such a huge job was impossible to accept. Still, as he made his way along the wall, he couldn't shake the feeling that some other memory was lingering at the edge of his thoughts, maybe even preparing to come to the surface. It was as if his mind was a vast ocean, and while dark scraps of knowledge had drifted to the darkness at the bottom, now one or two were starting to float back up.

"It's almost seven," he suddenly

remembered telling Alison a week or two earlier, "so there's not much point sleeping anymore. You said you have to go back to Peterborough today, so..." He remembered pausing, waiting for her to get the message. "I'm fine," he'd told her. "Everyone has nightmares, and that's all it was. You don't need to worry about me. Nothing bad is going to happen."

"I heard noises in the basement," he remembered her saying. "It was almost like..." She'd smiled, teasing him. "Let's take a look."

"No," he'd said firmly. "There's nothing down there."

And then, at some point, a scream. There had been a scream a little while later, maybe down in the basement itself. He looked around, but there was no sign of anything. He figured he had to be remembering dreams, that was all, but they seemed extremely vivid and as he stepped back and admired the breeze-block wall he couldn't stop thinking about the possibility that something important had happened, something he'd forgotten. He remembered his father investigating the wall during the previous night, pulling one of the blocks out and then -

And then...

He remembered dragging his father's unconscious body up the steps, but the rest of the night was something of a blur. It was as if dreams, memories and fantasies were colliding in his mind, and after a moment he realized he was developing a headache. Figuring that there was nothing to be gained by examining the wall any further, he turned and headed up the steps, before stopping to make doubly certain that the hatch was locked. After that, he grabbed his phone and brought up Alison's number, before trying to call her.

The call wouldn't even connect.

Setting his phone down, he made his way upstairs and headed to his grandmother's old room, which was bare now with even the carpet gone. He looked down at the spot where he'd found her body, and he tried to think back to what had happened next, but lately all his memories seemed to be patchy, with unexplained gaps. He'd dragged her onto the bed and then he'd called for an ambulance, or at least...

Pausing, he felt a lost memory detaching itself from his mind and starting to float upward, before a change in the current of his thoughts sent it drifting back down again.

Maybe, he figured, it would be good to get out of the house after all.

CHAPTER TWENTY-THREE

Today

"I'M SO GLAD you could meet me at such short notice," Sarah said with a smile as the waitress set some coffee cups between them. "It probably seems completely crazy that I'd contact you out of the blue like this."

"It's not crazy," Deborah Watkins replied, her eyes red from lack of sleep. As she reached down and picked up her cup, her hands were shaking. "I'm not even that surprised. I just... I guess I hoped that it ended when we moved out of that place."

"Like I told you on the phone," Sarah continued, "my husband and I aren't remotely upset or annoyed about anything. We're certainly not going to try to contest the sale, that's the farthest thing from our minds, it's just that we're interested in learning about your experiences while you were living in the house on Everley Street." She paused, waiting for an answer, but the other woman seemed lost in thought. "I understand that you and your husband lived there for only a couple of years before you sold up again?"

Deborah nodded.

"And after that, you only moved across town?"

"With Daisy," Deborah replied, turning and reaching over to the pram next to the table. She brushed her fingers against the child's hand, although Daisy didn't acknowledge the contact at all. Instead, the little girl seemed focused on Sarah, staring at her with unsettling blankness. For a child who was less than a year old, Daisy seemed preternaturally calm, apparently happy to just sit in her pram and not react to the world around her. A few minutes earlier, the waitress had dropped a tray of glasses; everyone in the cafe had been startled, but Daisy hadn't even blinked.

"She's beautiful," Sarah said with a smile.

Deborah shook her head.

"She is," Sarah continued. "She has such lovely blonde hair already."

"She's not right," Deborah whispered, with tears in her eyes, as she ran her fingers against the child's hands, as if she was still hoping that her daughter would look at her. "She hasn't been right since we left that house."

"The house on Everley Street?"

"I don't know if..." Turning to Sarah, Deborah paused for a moment. "I thought it'd be okay once we left. She was screaming so much, but I thought that once we got her out of there, it'd all somehow settle down. I know you probably think it was wrong of us to sell the place without mentioning any of the crazy things that had happened, but we were desperate. I mean, when your daughter's in some kind of pain, you'll do anything to get her out of there."

"I get it," Sarah replied, "I just... Can you tell me exactly what happened to you while you were living there? You said Daisy was screaming a lot."

"It was fine at first," Deborah explained, her voice trembling with fear. "We moved in, it was our first house and we were newly married, looking to start a family. Then when I became pregnant, we started to notice odd things happening. Little bumps, you know? Vibrations. Sometimes the glass in the kitchen window would start trembling slightly for no reason, and there'd be these faint whispers, and I started to feel ill at ease all the time, like I was never alone. We didn't believe in ghosts, neither of us did, but by the time Daisy was born we'd both started to wonder if maybe there was something..."

Her voice trailed off again.

"Something in the house with you?" Sarah asked.

"Please don't think we're crazy," Deborah whimpered, clearly struggling to keep from breaking down. "If it hadn't been for Daisy, we'd have stuck it out and laughed it all off, but after she was born... Everything was okay at the hospital, she seemed like the perfect baby, but once we got her home, she just didn't seem normal. Mike thought I was just suffering from depression after the birth, I mean he *said* he didn't think that, but I knew that's what was going through his mind. But after a few weeks, he started to notice it too. Daisy was strangely blank most of the time, and then other times she'd scream and scream."

Looking over at the child again, Sarah couldn't help but notice that she seemed to be staring.

"We took her to the doctor so many times," Deborah continued. "We're good parents, I swear, but they couldn't find anything wrong. Night after night, though, she was crying more and more, screaming... We tried having her in with us, but still she'd just scream in the middle of the night, and eventually it started happening during the day as well. Like she was in pain, but still we took her to the doctor almost every day and they couldn't find anything. I could see the look in their eyes, they thought we were paranoid, but I started thinking maybe it was..."

Sarah waited for her to finish. "Maybe it was what?"

"Maybe the pain wasn't physical," Deborah replied, leaning over and kissing her blank-faced, unresponsive daughter on the forehead. "Maybe it was emotional. Maybe she was sensing or seeing or hearing something that Mike and I weren't aware of."

"That sounds a little hard to believe," Sarah pointed out. "She's just a child."

"I know," Deborah continued, turning to her, "and Mike thought the same thing. He started accusing me of *wanting* Daisy to be sick, like he thought that I had some kind of mental illness. He'd hate it if he found out that I'd come to meet you today, he'd think it was part of it all, but I thought you deserved to know the truth. Finally, the night we left, that was when it all became too much and Daisy's screams... She wouldn't stop. She was screaming so much, she was turning blue and suffocating, she wasn't even drawing breath. I honestly believe that if we'd stayed in that house another few minutes, she'd have screamed herself to death."

"So you left?"

"In the middle of the night."

"Your husband finally accepted that it was really happening?"

"He had no choice. We put the house on the market the next day, and we decided we'd take a hit on it if we had to. We couldn't afford to lose money, but we also couldn't afford to stay. We saved up for so long to buy our first house, and now we're back to living at my mother's, but..." She paused again. "Please don't think we're bad people, but we decided not to mention any of the strange things that had happened. We needed a quick sale, we couldn't afford for it to take too long, and besides, we honestly thought there was a chance it wouldn't happen to anyone else." She took a deep breath. "Is that why you got in touch? Has something else happened there?"

Sarah paused. "Tell me about the basement."

Deborah shook her head, but it was clear that the mere mention of that word had brought fresh tears to her eyes. After a moment, she let out a brief, uncontrolled sob that left her a little breathless, as if she was on the verge of breaking down.

"I'm sorry," Sarah continued, "maybe we should -"

"No," Deborah stammered, finding more strength from somewhere, "please. Go on."

"The way you left the basement, it was

almost like you were too scared to go down there."

She nodded.

Sarah paused. "Can you... tell me *why* you were scared to go down there?"

"That's where it lives."

"Where what lives?"

"The evil. I don't know." Leaning forward, Deborah put her head in her hands for a moment. "If I tell you what I think, you'll laugh at me."

"I won't," Sarah replied. "I swear."

"I think something's down there," Deborah continued, looking at her again. "I don't know what, I don't know why, but I think something lives in that basement, and I think it's probably been living there for a very long time, and I think that somehow, for some reason, Daisy was more aware of it than the rest of us. Maybe it's because she's a child, but it seemed to get into her head and cause her pain. I think it extends through the whole house, but I'm certain it's rooted in that basement. One time, I had Daisy in my arms when I went down there to fetch something, and she cried so much and she actually tried to scratch my face, as if she was panicking." Another pause. "Have you been down there?"

Sarah nodded.

"Have you felt its presence?"

"I... No, I can't really say that I've felt anything in particular. It's kind of cold and spooky, but I certainly haven't felt anything that fits with what you've described."

"Do you have children?"

"They're at home with my husband right now."

"Get them out of there," Deborah said firmly. "Please, don't let the same thing happen to them."

Looking over at Daisy again, Sarah felt a chill at the sight of the baby's cold, dispassionate eyes. "Have you tried different doctors?" she asked finally, turning back to Deborah. "I know people in London who might be able to help, it's always worth getting someone to try again. If money's a problem, my husband and I can help."

Deborah shook her head.

"You can't give up on her," Sarah said firmly. "You have to try everything. There might be something simple that can be done to help her."

"Are you rich?" Deborah asked.

Sarah paused. "I... No, I mean, we're comfortable. My husband's a writer and I'm an estate lawyer."

"So you could afford to lose the house."

"What do you mean?"

"Burn it to the ground," Deborah replied. "Get the bricks taken away and pulverized, and make sure the basement is ripped out, then salt the earth and don't let another house get built there. We'd have done it ourselves, but we couldn't afford to take the hit. I still thought about doing it, but Mike said we had to be practical. I think he's still not quite convinced about what happened, but..." She reached across the table and took hold of Sarah's hands. "I don't know what's living in the basement, and I don't need to know. All that matters is getting rid of it."

"I -"

Before she could finish, Sarah spotted an angry-looking man storming past the window, headed for the door, and she immediately knew that it must be Deborah's husband.

"Promise me," Deborah hissed, as tears ran down her cheeks. "Burn that place and -"

"What the hell are you doing to my wife?" the man shouted, slamming the door open and hurrying to the table. Grabbing Deborah by the arm, he pulled her roughly up from her seat.

"Mike," she stammered, "it's okay -"

"What are you," Mike continued, glaring menacingly at Sarah, "some kind of psychic? A journalist? Keep the hell away from us or I swear to God I'll make you pay!"

"I'm none of those things," Sarah replied, shocked by his fury, "I just -"

"I don't care!" he shouted, pushing her back against the wall. The cafe's few other customers were staring in shock, and the waitress had a phone in her hand, as if she was considering calling the police. "This family has been through enough and I won't have anyone starting it all up again!"

"She's the new owner of the house," Deborah told him, trying to pull her husband back. "Mike, please, I was just trying to warn her!"

"You own that place now?" Mike asked breathlessly.

Sarah nodded.

"Then God help you," he replied, taking a step back before angrily grabbing the pram and starting to wheel it toward the door. "If you want my advice, you'll steer clear of the place. Don't even think about taking legal action, though. I've spoken to lawyers, I know we didn't do anything wrong. There's nothing you can do, it's your house now."

"I'm sorry," Deborah sobbed, following her husband to the door. She turned back to Sarah. "Protect your family. Whatever else happens, whatever anyone says to you, protect your family or -"

Before she could finish, Mike grabbed her by the arm and pulled her outside. Stunned, Sarah stood and watched as he marched Deborah and Daisy toward the car park. Finally, she reached into her pocket and took out her phone, quickly bringing up John's number.

"What's up?" he said as soon as he answered. "You on your way back yet?"

"Sure," she replied cautiously, "but... Is

everything okay?"

There was a pause on the other end of the line. "Yeah," he said after a moment, as if the question had unsettled him. "Why, what's wrong?"

"Nothing," she replied, as she saw Mike driving Deborah and Daisy away. "Nothing," she said again, "I just... I'll be back soon. I need to talk to you about something important."

***

"Great," he muttered as he set his phone back onto the window ledge. Turning, he looked across the garden, and for a moment he couldn't help thinking back to the greenhouse that had once stood a few meters away, filled with his grandmother's prize fuchsias. The greenhouse was long gone now, of course, and apart from its basic dimensions the garden was pretty much unrecognizable.

"John?" a voice called out suddenly, from the other side of the fence. "John Myers, is that you?"

He barely had time to recognize the voice before he saw an old man's face popping up over the fence with a smile. It had been twenty years since John had last seen that face, but nevertheless he knew it immediately.

"Mr. Shepherd," he said with a polite smile, making his way over to the fence and reaching up so he could shake the man's hand. "I was going to knock on your door later and see how you're doing."

"I heard voices," Mr. Shepherd replied, "and I couldn't believe it when I realized it was you. How long's it been? Ten, fifteen years?"

"Twenty."

"Twenty?" At this, the old man's eyes nearly popped out of his head. "Lord have mercy, it doesn't feel like more than a month or two since I came into your garden to moan about that huge bonfire you had burning."

"I remember that."

"What are you doing back here? You're not the one who's bought the damn place, are you?"

"I am," John replied. "I don't even know why, really. I guess I was just being a little sentimental."

"Well, you won't find that much has changed in the area," Mr. Shepherd continued. "I'm still here, for one thing. Still not got my compost heap sorted, either. You know, I can't think what I've really been doing with my time over the past two decades. Just pottering about, going from one little job that needs fixing to another. Nothing to report, really. Meanwhile, you went out and became a famous writer."

"I wouldn't say famous," John replied. "I do okay."

"And you're married, aren't you? With kids?"

"I am, yes."

"Where are they? I bet they look just like you."

"They're playing somewhere," he replied. "Back in the house, I think. You know what kids are like."

***

"Quiet!" Scott hissed to Katie as he gently pulled the hatch down, leaving them in darkness at the top of the steps that led down to the basement. "If Dad finds out we're down here, he'll kill us."

"Dad wouldn't kill us."

"It's an expression, dumb-ass. It just means he'd be mad."

"Dad isn't mad."

Scott sighed. "It's another expression. He'd be angry."

"Oh." Katie paused. "Why?"

"I don't know, he's just funny about the basement for some reason."

"Why?"

"I told you, I don't know."

"But why?"

"Stop asking dumb questions," he replied, using the torch app on his father's phone to light the way as he began to make his way down the creaking steps. "Are you coming or not?"

"Wait for me!" she called out, hurrying after him.

"Sssh!" he hissed, turning to her again. "Can you just be quiet for five minutes?"

"Don't yell at me."

"Come on," he said with a sigh, heading down to the foot of the steps and then shining the light around. "It stinks down here. I swear to God, it's like something's rotten."

"Why would something be rotten down here?" Katie asked.

"I don't know." He crouched down and cautiously poked at one of the damp cardboard boxes. "Maybe someone left food down here or something."

"I think we should go back up."

"What's wrong?" he asked with a smile. "Scared?"

"No!"

"Then why do you want to go back up?"

"I just don't want to get into trouble, that's all."

"Why's it so small down here?" Scott asked suddenly, stopping and looking toward the far wall.

"It's not *that* small," Katie whispered.

"It's smaller than upstairs," he continued, "and that wall's different to the others. It's like it was put in much later." He took a step forward, before Katie grabbed his arm.

"Don't!" she hissed.

"Whatever," he replied, pulling free and heading to the wall. He reached out and ran his right hand over the surface, feeling the roughness of the breeze blocks. After a moment, he turned his head and leaned closer, as if he was listening out for something.

Katie waited, fighting the urge to run back upstairs.

"Hey," Scott said after a moment, "come over here and listen to this."

"Listen to what?" she asked cautiously.

"Just come and listen."

"Tell me what it is first."

"I don't know what it is, it's like -" He paused, frowning as he listened some more. "It comes and goes, but it's like a scratching sound."

Katie instinctively took a step back. "Do you think it's rats?"

"Come and listen."

"I don't like rats."

"It's not rats!"

She opened her mouth to ask again, before realizing that she was in danger of coming across like a scared little girl. Which, to be fair, she was, but still... She didn't want to seem weak in front of her brother. Swallowing hard, she took a few steps forward and then leaned closer, placing her ear against the cold, damp wall.

"Wait," Scott whispered.

"For what?"

"For the noise, dumb-ass."

"But what -"

Before she could finish, she heard a faint scrabbling sound from the other side.

"That's no rat," Scott told her.

"Then what is it?"

"I don't know. It seems kind of muffled, though."

"We should tell Mum and Dad," Katie continued. "They'll know what to do."

"You're such a baby," he replied, making his way past her as he examined the wall. "You *always* want to go and get Mum and Dad."

"I do not!"

"Do too."

"I'm going to tell Mum you said that!"

"Loser," he said with a smile, before crouching down and taking a look at one of the breeze blocks. "This part isn't sealed the same as the rest. Do you think we could get through?"

"Why would we want to go through?"

He rolled his eyes. "To see what's on the other side, dumb-ass. I think there's another part to this basement, and it's been sealed off for some reason."

"And that's where the rats are?"

"Yeah." He paused. "If they *are* rats."

"But..." She frowned. "If there's something, and if someone sealed it off, isn't that a good thing? Why would we want to risk letting it out?"

"To see what it is."

"But what if it's rats?"

"Then they'll bite your face off," he said with a smile. "Do you know how violent and mean a hungry rat can get?"

"Stop it."

"And do you know how *big* they can be? I heard about rats that are as big as cats."

"Scott, stop it!"

"Maybe," he continued, "just a few centimeters away on the other side of this wall, there's a rat as big as a -"

Before he could finish, they both heard the hatch opening, and they spun around just in time to see John hurrying down the stairs with a flashlight in his hand.

"Dad!" Scott called out. "We -"

"Out!" John shouted, grabbing them both and pulling them back toward the stairs. "What the hell do you think you're doing here?"

"You're hurting me!" Katie shouted.

"Get out of here!" he yelled, pushing them at the steps and then shoving them as hard as he could back up toward the hatch. "Jesus Christ, I leave you alone for five minutes and you start disobeying strict orders not to come down here!"

"We just wanted to see," Scott replied. "Dad, I think we found -"

"Out!" John said again, as the three of them reached the kitchen. Turning, he slammed the hatch shut and then slid the bolt across before turning to them. "Okay, so whose idea was it to go down there, huh?"

"Dad -" Scott began.

"Whose idea was it?" he shouted.

"Mine!" Scott replied, back up against the wall. "What's so wrong about going down there anyway?"

"You were given a direct order to keep out!"

"It's just a stupid basement!"

"It might be dangerous down there," he said firmly. "There might be wild animals, there might be anything! Fumes, poison, traps -"

"We heard a noise."

"No," John replied, shaking his head, "you didn't."

"We did," Katie whispered.

"There's nothing down there," John said firmly, "do you understand me? I want both of you to tell me that you understand, right now! And don't go telling your mother all these crazy stories, you'll only end up worrying her."

Katie looked at Scott, waiting to follow his

lead.

"Why are you being like this?" Scott asked his father. "I get that we weren't allowed down there, but it's *just* a basement." He waited for an answer. "Isn't it?"

For a moment, John seemed almost on the verge of striking his son, so great was his anger. Finally, however, he took a step back, as if his rage had passed its peak, although there was still a hint of white hot fury in his eyes.

"We're going to the carnival tonight," he told them, "and we're going to have to head out as soon as your mother gets home, so why don't you two go upstairs and get ready?"

"Dad -" Katie began.

"Now!" he shouted.

Scott muttered something under his breath as he and Katie hurried through to the hallway, leaving John alone in the kitchen to listen to the sound of his children running to the bedroom. Sighing, he turned and looked down at the hatch that led to the basement, and after a moment he realized that although he still felt furious, he couldn't remember *why* he was so angry. He leaned against the counter and closed his eyes, feeling the anger swirling in his mind, and then -

Suddenly it was gone. He felt calm again, and when he opened his eyes it was almost as if he was someone else entirely. He didn't even remember why he'd been so angry, and he didn't really *want* to remember. All he knew was that he couldn't allow anyone to go down to the basement. Not ever.

CHAPTER TWENTY-FOUR

Twenty years ago

AFTER PULLING THE DOOR SHUT, John paused for a moment with the key in his hand. He knew this was an important moment, that he was finally leaving the house for the last time, but something was holding him back. His bags were packed and he was traveling light as he headed off to the train station, bound for Bristol and for the house his father had bought for his time at university. Still, he felt as if he'd forgotten something.

Opening the door again, he stepped back into the kitchen and looked around, before heading to the hatch and pulling it open. There was something in the basement, something invisible and silent that seemed to be calling him, but as he made his way down the steps and used his phone to light the way ahead, he realized that he still couldn't see anything untoward. The breeze-block wall had drawn no unusual comments from the surveyor who'd assessed the house during the same process, and although he'd been down to inspect the cramped space several times over the previous few weeks, John still had no idea why he felt drawn to the place.

He stopped and waited.

Listening.

There seemed to be a scream in the air, yet the basement itself was silent. For a moment, he could almost imagine a figure on the other side of the wall, slamming its fists against the blocks and begging to be let out. At the same time, he couldn't hear a thing. He figured he'd been alone in the house for long enough, and that his imagination had begun to run wild.

Time to go.

Heading back up to the hatch, he told himself that he needed to be strong, that he was in danger of getting too sentimental. Even though he wanted to once again go down to the basement and search, he forced himself to close the hatch and slide the bolt across, and then to head to the door. Stepping outside, he pulled the door shut and this time he wasted no time in slipping the key into the lock. Finally, after hauling his bag onto his shoulder, he headed to the street and stopped, before looking back at the house one final time.

He felt a shiver pass through his body as he realized that he'd most likely never see the place again.

"Goodbye," he whispered, looking at the bedroom window and half expecting to see his grandmother's ghost staring down at him. But, of course, she wasn't there. There was no such thing as ghosts, he knew that now.

CHAPTER TWENTY-FIVE

Today

"WOW!" SARAH SAID, laughing as she saw another float coming past, this time with a large model of a windmill lit up against the night sky. "That's the best one yet!"

The carnival had been running for almost an hour now but showed no signs of stopping. Marching bands played as trucks pulled large, decorated trailers along the seafront road, and a large crowd of several thousand people had turned out to watch the procession as it made its way slowly past the castle and then along the promenade toward the fun fair that had fetched up in town for the summer. Street vendors were selling burgers and hot-dogs, while every twenty feet or so there were clowns selling balloons.

"Katie," Sarah continued, nudging her daughter's shoulder, "can you see properly? Do you want me to lift you up?"

"It's okay," Katie replied, clearly not enjoying herself very much as she watched a huge plastic swan being driven past, with three teenaged girls sitting on the back wearing white dresses and crowns.

"Come on," Sarah said, picking her up anyway and lifting her so she could see better. "I bet you've never seen anything like this, huh?"

"It's pretty weird," Katie muttered.

"So what's wrong?" Sarah asked. "You and Scott have seemed off ever since I got back from town earlier."

Katie turned to her.

"Did something happen?" Sarah asked cautiously.

"Dad got really mad at us," Katie replied, as another marching band made its way past.

"What did you do?"

"Nothing. We just went down into the basement."

"By yourselves?"

"I know we weren't supposed to, but Dad got *really* angry. I thought he was going to hit us."

"Your father would never do that," Sarah told her, as she spotted John and Scott making their way back through the crowd with candy floss. "You know that, right?"

"I suppose."

"This is lame," Scott said he reached them, rolling his eyes. "I can't believe people actually pretend they enjoy it."

"To be fair," John told him, "I used to think it was lame when I was your age too. It's only now that I can really appreciate it in all its tacky glory."

"Do you want an ice cream?" Sarah asked Katie, hoping to cheer her daughter up a little.

Katie shook her head.

"A balloon?"

"No thank you."

"Well you have to have something."

"Can you put me down on the ground? My legs are aching."

Setting Katie down, Sarah paused for a moment before turning to John. "So I heard you got pretty mad at the kids earlier when they went into the basement."

"It was nothing."

"I think you freaked Katie out."

"That's not exactly difficult. The kid's jumpy as hell."

"Okay," Sarah replied, a little shocked by his attitude, "that's new. What crawled up *your* butt and died?"

"I just told them not to go down there and

they disobeyed me, that's all. I thought we were supposed to be instilling a little respect in their minds?"

"We are, but..." Pausing, she realized that something seemed a little different about her husband, as if he was harsher and less tolerant. He'd always been more lenient with the children, yet any mention of the basement was clearly enough to get him riled. "This place isn't good for you, is it?" she asked finally. "This whole town, I mean. I didn't understand before, but I see it now."

"It's not the town. It's just the way the kids disobeyed me."

Spotting a dark mark on his neck, she leaned closer. "Did you burn yourself?"

He quickly pulled his collar up. "It's nothing."

She opened her mouth to ask again, but she knew her husband well enough to realize that he was clamming up. "I met the people who sold the house earlier," she continued finally. "I got their names from Reginald and I arranged to meet them in a cafe."

He turned to her. "Without telling me?"

"You said you didn't want to bother."

"I didn't mean for you to go behind my back."

"Calm down," she replied, "I just met the woman, Deborah Watkins, for a cup of tea and a chat. She had some interesting things to say about that house."

"Such as?"

"Do you know that she and her husband were basically driven out of the place? From what she said, it's clear she thinks the house is haunted and -"

"Rubbish."

"I saw her daughter," Sarah continued, as another float drove past blaring loud music. "They have this one-year-old baby and she's kind of catatonic. Deborah said that the girl screamed and screamed on the night they left, and she said she thought... Well, I know you'll think this sounds crazy, but she said she thought there was something living in the basement."

John rolled his eyes.

"I'm serious," Sarah told him. "She wasn't making it up, she definitely believed it."

"Then she's obviously nuts. It's probably postpartum depression, something like that."

"Have *you* ever noticed anything in the basement?"

"I've barely been down there."

"And yet you act like a maniac when the kids dare to take a look."

"I told you -"

"I don't believe in ghosts," she replied, interrupting him. "You know that, I've always been like that and it's still true, but there are a lot of weird things pointing at that basement right now. I'm not making any grand claims, but..." She paused for a moment. "I'm just glad we're getting out of here tomorrow. I know it was my idea to stay, but with the way things have been going -"

"Actually, I think I might stick around for a few more days."

She stared at him, barely able to believe what he'd just said. "What?"

"I have a few things to do. You and the kids should go back to London, but I want to stay in the house a little while longer." A passing float lit up his face and he smiled. "Look at that one," he continued, as if he was trying to change the subject. "Are they supposed to be ants or butterflies? It's kinda hard to tell."

"John -"

"Can't I have a little time by myself?" He kept his eyes on the passing float, as the flashing lights bathed his face in red light, then yellow, then white, then back to red again.

Sarah paused, worried by the sudden change in her husband's demeanor. In less than twenty-four hours they'd switched positions, and now she was the one who wanted to leave while he preferred to stick around.

"John," she said finally, "I really think -"

"Let's go get you an ice cream," John said

suddenly, grabbing Katie's hand. "Come on, you always love ice cream, and I really could do with not being nagged for a few minutes."

"Nagged?" Sarah said, shocked by his tone.

"I don't want an ice cream right now," Katie replied.

"Of course you do."

"I think she's okay," Sarah said. "John, let's just watch the rest of the carnival."

"Well, *I* want an ice cream," he continued, "and I'd like to take Katie with me. Is that okay? We came down here to have fun, right? So let's have fun instead of going on and on about things."

She opened her mouth to argue with him, before realizing that there was no point. Instead, she watched as he led a reluctant Katie away through the crowd. He seemed nervous and on edge, as if he couldn't stay still for more than a few minutes at a time.

"What's wrong with Dad?" Scott asked.

She turned to look at him, as another marching band passed in the street nearby.

"Nothing," she said after moment, forcing a smile. "Nothing's wrong with him, he's just finding it a little odd to be back in his hometown, that's all. Don't worry, this time tomorrow we'll be back in London and everything'll be back to normal."

***

"John!" she called out a couple of hours later, making her way across the garbage-strewn street that was still waiting for council sweepers to arrive now that the parade was over. "John! Katie! Where are you?"

The carnival had died down an hour ago and the crowd had dispersed quickly, while the fun fair had shut down and the beach area was now mostly empty except for a few scattered groups of people hanging out in the shadows. So far, however, there was no sign of either John or Katie, and although she kept telling herself not to worry about the fact that her husband wasn't answering his phone, Sarah couldn't shake the feeling in her gut that something didn't feel quite right.

"Dad!" Scott shouted, a few steps further back. "Katie!"

"Come on," Sarah muttered, taking her phone from her pocket and trying his number again, still to no avail. "Are you trying to make some kind of point?" she wondered out loud, turning and looking both ways along the street. "Is that what this is?"

"Maybe they're down by the water," Scott suggested.

"We already checked there."

"Yeah, but maybe we missed them before."

She turned to him.

"Where else should we look?" he asked with a shrug.

"Maybe they just went home," she pointed out.

"Without telling us?"

"Maybe your father lost his phone, and then he couldn't find us in the crowd."

"We didn't move from where we were when he left."

"Well, it must be something like that," she replied, starting to feel exasperated. She kept telling herself not to panic, that Katie was absolutely fine with John, but at the same time she also felt as if her husband seemed a little different, as if he was holding something back. "We'll check the beach one more time and then we should head back to the house. We'll probably find them back in the kitchen, laughing about the fact that we spent so long out here looking for them."

"You don't really think that," Scott said.

"Yes, I do. They probably just think this is a game."

Forty-five minutes later, having checked the beach and the promenade a couple more times, Sarah and Scott finally got back to the house, and they both noticed immediately that all the lights were off.

"I don't think they're here," Scott said cautiously.

"They probably just went to bed," Sarah replied, although she felt as if she was clutching at straws. She checked her phone again, to make sure that John hadn't tried calling her back, before leading Scott to the front door and taking the key from her pocket. Her hands were trembling slightly, but she knew she couldn't let her fear show too much. "Come on, there's nothing to worry about. They can't have gone far."

They spent the next few minutes looking around the house, only to find no sign of either John or Katie. Although she tried to hide her concern so that Scott wouldn't worry, Sarah was feeling increasingly worried by the time she got back down to the kitchen. She checked her phone yet again, while trying to work out what circumstances would cause John to ignore a dozen calls.

"We've checked everywhere, then," she muttered. "They must still be out. I guess they found something fun to do."

"We haven't checked *everywhere*," Scott pointed out, turning to look at the hatch that led down to the basement.

"Why would they be down there?"

He shrugged.

Sighing, she realized he was right.

"Wait here," she told him, heading to the hatch and lifting it up, before looking down into the darkness below. She knew it was crazy, but in the pit of her stomach she felt a strong desire to *not* go down the steps. "John?" she called out. "Katie?"

Silence.

"There's a hidden part down there," Scott said suddenly.

She turned to him.

"There *is*," he continued. "Katie and I found it earlier, just before Dad caught us. We didn't ask him about it because he was so mad, but there's a false wall and everything."

"Don't be ridiculous," she replied, "why -"

"I'll *show* you," he said, slipping past her and making his way down the stairs.

"Scott, don't go down there!"

"Why not? Because Dad says we can't? Are you scared of him too?"

"I'm not scared of him, I just..." She paused, before activating the flashlight on her phone and starting to follow him down. "At least let me go first," she continued. "Scott, seriously, there's no hidden room down here, the idea's completely absurd."

"Come and see for yourself," he replied. "I know what we found."

Leading her across the basement, he stopped when he reached the far wall. As soon as he turned his head and pressed his ear against the wall, he could hear the faint scratching sound from before, and a moment later he saw from the shocked look in her eyes that his mother could hear it too.

"Now do you believe me?" he whispered.

Stepping back, Sarah shone the flashlight across the wall. She wanted to tell Scott that he was imagining things, that there was no way there could be a hidden room in the basement, but as the scratching sound continued she was starting to realize that whatever was on the other side, it was definitely real.

"Go upstairs," she said finally.

"Why?"

"Go upstairs and wait for me." She frowned as the flashlight picked out a section of brickwork that looked different to the rest, as if it could be moved aside. "Scott, don't argue with me, go upstairs."

"Are you going to try to get through?" he asked. "I found it, that means I should get to come with you!"

"Scott," she said firmly, with her eyes still fixed on the brickwork, "I'm your mother and I'm telling you to go upstairs and wait for me. I'll be two minutes."

Sighing, he headed to the steps, before glancing back at her.

"What if Dad comes home?" he asked cautiously.

"Then..." She paused. "Just go upstairs and wait."

Clearly annoyed, Scott made his way loudly up the stairs, stomping on each step. When he reached the top, however, he ducked down and instead of going through the hatch he settled to watch his mother from the darkness.

Stepping closer to the brickwork in the corner, Sarah reached out and found that this section of the wall wobbled slightly, as if it wasn't properly secure. She put her phone in her mouth, holding it so the flashlight shone straight ahead, before fumbling with the brickwork and finding that it could be pushed into the wall. There was a faint grinding sound as she pushed further, and then she heard some kind of mechanism coming to life on the other side. A narrow, low doorway was opening in the wall, and after a moment she felt cold air against her hands. She leaned down and looked through the gap, and now the scratching sound was much louder than before.

Up on the stairs, Scott watched in horror as his mother bent down and began to crawl inside.

"Please come back," he whispered, shaking with fear. "Please..."

Taking the phone from her mouth, Sarah scrambled to her feet on the other side of the wall and shone the flashlight around. She was in a large, dark room, a second part of the basement, and after a moment the flashlight fell across a set of bones on the floor. Shocked, she stared down and saw that the bones included a full human body, complete with some kind of metal pole screwed to the spine, along with a skull that had been cracked open at the back. The jawbone had been pulled away and was over in the corner. Telling herself that it had to be fake, that there was some obvious explanation she was missing, she spotted more bones nearby before turning and shining the flashlight toward the source of the scratching sound.

She froze, unable to believe what she was seeing.

In the middle of the room, there was a dark-haired girl tied and bound on a table. She was tugging at the ropes and chains that secured her, causing the scratching sound as she did so, and a thick gag had been tied around her face, covering her mouth. One of her hands had been worked free, and she was waving what appeared to be a corkscrew toward the darker end of the room, while trying desperately to say something despite the gag.

"No," Sarah whispered, taking a step back. "This isn't real."

The girl on the table tried again to speak, sounding even more desperate this time.

"Jesus," Sarah continued, rushing forward and starting to untie the gag with trembling fingers. "What the hell's going on down here?"

"Gah!" the girl gasped as soon as the gag was away. "You really took your time, didn't you?"

"Who are you?"

"Untie me."

"But -"

"Untie me before she comes back for another shot!"

"Before who comes back?" Sarah asked, turning to the darkness all around. "What is this place?"

"This place," the girl replied, "is your husband's sick little invention, and *she* isn't going to hold back for much longer, so get me out of here!"

"What do you -"

Before she could finish, Sarah heard a scrabbling sound nearby. She turned and looked toward the far wall, but when she held the flashlight out, the girl pushed her hand away.

"No light," she hissed. "I don't know how she'd respond to light. It might make her angry."

"Who?" Sarah asked.

"Who do you think? John's grandmother."

"John's grandmother died twenty years ago," Sarah replied, trembling with fear as the scrabbling sound continued.

"Says who?" the girl asked. "John? Anyone else? 'Cause John seems like a pretty unreliable witness right now. Can you please untie me? I don't know if I can fend her off with this corkscrew for much longer."

Sarah paused for a moment, staring in horror

at the girl, before starting to loosen the ropes around her legs and arms. "I don't know who you are," she stammered, "or what's happening down here, but my husband -"

"Has some serious mental problems," the girl replied. "Oh, and my name's Hannah, and you're welcome. You can thank me later."

"For what?"

"For all the help I'm going to give you." As soon as she was able to pull her hands free, Hannah put the corkscrew between her teeth and started slipping the ropes from around her ankles. She muttered something, but the fork meant it was impossible to make out any words.

"There has to be an explanation for this," Sarah replied, pulling the last of the ropes away. "It doesn't make any sense."

"There *is* a explanation," Hanna replied. "Your husband is a very sick man with some serious -"

She stopped suddenly, before turning and swinging the corkscrew wildly toward the darkness, just as a human shape appeared briefly and then receded back into the shadows.

"What the hell was that?" Sarah asked, stepping back against the wall.

"I told you," Hannah continued, finally able to climb down off the table. Keeping the corkscrew held out, she stepped toward Sarah. "That was

John's grandmother. The one who was supposed to have died twenty years ago."

"But she *did* die," Sarah replied. "Everyone knows she died."

"Oh yeah?" Hannah said, as they both watched a figure shuffling toward them through the darkness. "Then tell me who *that* is, because I can promise you one thing." She held out her wrist to show Sarah a fresh bite mark. "It's sure as hell not a ghost."

CHAPTER TWENTY-SIX

Today

"SOUND-PROOFED ROOM," Hannah explained a moment later, as she and Sarah reached the other part of the basement and hurried toward the stairs. "At least, that's what he tried to do, but it wouldn't have worked, not if the old woman had been cable of making more than a few scratches. Fortunately for John, she was too weak after the stroke. There's a full hidden section down here, though, with a surprisingly sophisticated door. I've got to admit, I'm slightly impressed by what your husband was able to put together all by himself when he was still, what, a teenager?"

"That wasn't John's grandmother," Sarah replied, stopping at the foot of the stairs and looking back toward the hidden door. She could still hear movement on the other side of the false wall. "It can't be."

"I wish we could work out how to get the door closed again," Hannah said. "There must be a lever somewhere, but I don't fancy searching for it, not with the old dear still on the loose. I kept her at bay with the corkscrew, but she never gives up. I guess she's hungry for something other than rat meat."

Sarah turned to her. "That is *not* my husband's grandmother in there! My husband's grandmother is dead!"

"Maybe he thought she was dead at first," Hannah explained, "when he first found her on the floor of her room twenty years ago, but in case you never noticed, John Myers is a slightly weird kind of guy. For starters, there's no record of his grandmother's death, and do you know why? Because he never called anyone after he found her. No police, no ambulance, no funeral home, no nothing. Instead, he brought her down here to the basement."

Sarah shook her head, unable to believe what she was hearing.

"I don't think he even remembers that he did it," Hannah continued. "He brought her down here, and he partitioned off a section of the basement, he even tried to sound-proof it. Pretty impressive for a kid working alone, but then I guess he's always been a smart guy. Some people just have a knack for this. He probably thought it was his own way of burying her, but whatever was wrong with her, she began to recover. I'd love to have seen his face when he realized she wasn't dead fter all."

"But where has she been for the past twenty years?"

"In there," Hannah replied.

"That's impossible. Other people have lived here since."

"And they almost went nuts," Hannah continued. "John's grandmother Elizabeth suffered a massive stroke twenty years ago, and probably several more strokes after that, which left her almost completely immobile. She couldn't talk, couldn't call for help, couldn't even bang on the walls, so the most anyone heard was a faint bumping sound, just enough to make them think the place was haunted. It took me a while to figure out how the old dear managed to stay alive, but there was just enough air getting through, and food was coming down through gaps in the wall."

Sarah turned to her.

"It was a one-in-a-million chance," Hannah explained, "but the guy next door has a compost heap that leaks through the soil, and that compost heap happens to encourage rats, and rats get pretty big and meaty. They found herself down here, and voila! Night of the living grandmother!"

"That's impossible," Sarah replied, trying to stay calm. "An old woman can't live in darkness for twenty years, with no-one noticing, living on rats and drinking, what, rainwater that leaks through? The idea's insane."

"No," Hannah replied, "it's highly, highly, *highly* unlikely, but then I only get sent to check out cases that are a little off the wall. I wouldn't even have believed it if I hadn't seen it for myself. Thousands of people die on this planet every day and almost all of them go according to plan. Very occasionally, however, one gets complicated and I'm sent to -"

They both turned as they heard a bumping sound from the other side of the wall.

"This might not be much of a surprise to you at this point," Hannah continued, "but I don't think the old woman's in a very good mood. She can just about walk. Not fast, but she can do it."

"Mum?"

Turning, Sarah saw to her horror that Scott was watching from the top of the stairs.

"Get into the kitchen!" she shouted, hurrying toward him and manhandling him through the hatch. "I told you to wait up there for me!"

"Is there really an old woman in the basement?" he asked, before staring in shock as Hannah followed them up. "Who's she?"

"She's -" Sarah paused, before turning to Hannah. "I... I mean, she's -" Another pause. "Who *are* you?"

"I'm here to help straighten this mess out," Hannah told them as she closed the hatch. "This is the kind of thing I deal with, deaths that haven't quite gone according to plan. Of course, I couldn't just rock up and ask John what was happening, he wouldn't have been able to tell me. His mind is basically divided in two, just like the basement. The normal John Myers, the guy you two know, has no memory of entombing his grandmother down there. The other side of him remembers, though, and sometimes it takes over, but only when it's needed, when it has to do something to maintain the illusion. There are a couple of dead bodies in the basement, I'm pretty sure that back in the day, a couple of people found out what had happened and he killed them. Not that he remembers doing that, most likely, but it happened. And his grandmother apparently ended up eating their meat, which is particularly pleasant."

"No," Sarah said firmly. "None of this is possible."

"He's always been scared of his grandmother's ghost lingering in this place," Hannah continued. "That was his subconscious mind reminding him that she wasn't really gone. It's also why, without really knowing the cause, he felt compelled to buy the house back. As for the other families who lived here, I'm sure they heard just enough faint bumps in the night to start worrying about the house being haunted, and the human imagination took over from there. Babies are the most open to traumatic emotions, so any child who lived in this house would have sensed the horror much more clearly and..." She paused. "Well, that wouldn't have ended well."

"Where's Dad?" Scott asked. "Where's Katie?"

"I don't know," Sarah replied, pulling him closer and holding him tight, "but when we find him, he'll straighten all of this out. He'll tell us what's really happening."

"I already told you what's really happening," Hannah told her. "You just need to pay more attention."

"My husband is not a monster!" Sarah shouted, with tears in her eyes.

"No," Hannah replied, "he's not, but there's definitely another side to him. I saw that other side a few nights ago, when I talked my way into spending the night here. When he led me into the basement, something changed in him. I could see it in his eyes, the other John took over. That was when he briefly remembered what had happened. Fortunately, I already had my suspicions so I'd armed myself with a corkscrew. He overpowered me, but at least the corkscrew allowed me to fend the old dear off while I worked out how to escape. I was just starting to get a little worried, but fortunately you guys showed up."

"You've been down there for days?" Sarah asked.

"She's cautious and scared," Hannah explained. "A good swipe with the corkscrew usually made her stay away for a few hours at a time. I could hear her eating rats, though. Crunching on their bones, sucking as much blood as she could from their little corpses. Not pleasant."

Sarah shook her head.

"You don't believe me?" Hannah asked.

"I don't believe any of this!" Sarah shouted. "My husband's grandmother is dead, she's not -"

Before she could finish, there was a knocking sound from the other side of the hatch, and the door shuddered a little. Just as it was about to open, however, Hannah stamped her foot down, keeping it shut, and slid the bolt across.

"You were saying?" she asked.

"Mummy, I'm scared," Scott whimpered, hiding behind Sarah. "What's down there?"

"I don't know," Sarah replied, staring in horror as the hatch continued to shudder. "I... This can't be happening..."

"People do weird stuff all the time," Hannah continued. "John's not the first odd teenager. In his case, however, he's also got a pretty wild imagination, perhaps he had some luck along the way, and the unusual circumstances meant he was able to get away with it." She paused for a moment. "There's no grave for his grandmother. No record of a funeral. John's father owned the house back when they lived here, so it's not like anyone else came and disturbed things when the old woman disappeared. John was able to fob people off, to claim his grandmother had been buried somewhere else. Why would anyone question him? He was all alone, just trying to survive, and I'm pretty sure that his head had been messed with from an early age. Someone should have caught on and realized what was going on, but no-one did. He was lucky, or unlucky, depending on how you want to look at it."

"He always said his grandmother was an awful woman," Sarah stammered, staring down at the hatch. "He said she was cruel and mean."

"I believe him," Hannah replied. "A little nature, a little nurture, and John's mind literally divided in two."

"My husband isn't mad," Sarah told her. "He isn't!"

"Yeah, well -" The hatch trembled again, as the old woman continued to try forcing it open from the other side. "We can debate the precise treatment plan required to get John back to full health later. Right now, we have to -"

"He has Katie," Sarah said suddenly.

"Who?"

"Our other daughter. We were all at the carnival, and then suddenly he and Katie disappeared."

"How long ago?"

"A few hours now, but he'd never do anything to hurt her. He loves her, he loves us all."

"Has he seemed different lately?" Hannah asked. "Short-tempered, maybe? Angrier?"

"A little, but I assumed that was just because he was back here."

"And coming back here has reopened the scar tissue between the two sides of his mind," Hannah continued. "I'm sure you're right, I'm sure he'd never intentionally hurt your daughter, but we still need to find them before he *unintentionally* hurts her. Your husband is very unstable right now." She looked around for a moment. "I had a bag with me the other night. Have you seen a small, red satchel anywhere?"

"I -"

"Never mind," she continued, "he probably put it in the trash so he wouldn't have to see it. Come here for a moment."

"Mummy, I don't want to be in this house," Scott sobbed, pulling on Sarah's sleeve.

"I know, sweetheart," she replied, "we're going to -"

"Come here!" Hannah hissed, grabbing Sarah's arm and pulling her onto the hatch, before stepping back. "Just keep pushing down so the old woman can't come up. I'm going to look for my bag, it's got some things in it that I need. I'll be back in a couple of minutes and then we can figure out how to find John and your daughter."

"But -"

"Just keep a cool head," Hannah said firmly, hurrying to the door. "And keep that hatch shut! Whatever John's grandmother might have been like before, she's just spent twenty years alone in the dark. Her mind must be gone by now."

"Wait!" Sarah called out to her, but it was already too late and Hannah had disappeared through to another part of the house. A moment later, the hatch shuddered again, and Sarah had to push down harder to make sure that it stayed shut since the bolt was already coming loose.

"Who's in the basement?" Scott asked, squeezing his mother's hand tight.

"I..." Looking down at the hatch, Sarah paused for a moment. "It's no-one, sweetie. It's nothing. Just stay calm, everything's going to be okay."

"And who's the other woman? Who's the one who came up with you?"

"I... I have no idea." Feeling a rising sense of panic, Sarah quickly reminded herself that she had to stay calm for her family's sake. There'd be time to sob and break down later, but right now she had to take charge and somehow find a way through the insanity. "It's all going to be fine," she continued, forcing a smile. "Trust me."

"She's talking," Scott replied, looking at the hatch.

"What?"

"The person down there," he continued, his eyes wide with horror. "I can hear her whispering something."

"No," Sarah said, "that's not -" Before she could finish, however, she realized he was right. Staying quiet for a moment, she listened to a faint, muttered whisper that was coming from the other side of the hatch, accompanied by a scratching sound.

"What's she saying?" Scott asked, stepping back against the wall.

"I don't know," Sarah replied, before leaning down slightly.

"Help me," the old woman's voice could just about be heard saying, although her voice was dry and rough. "Please, let me out of here. I've been in the dark for so long."

Sarah opened her mouth to reply, but no words came out.

"Is she evil?" Scott whispered.

"I..." Sarah paused. "She's just an old..."

"Please," the voice continued, slurred and damaged, "help me..."

"Don't," Scott said firmly, his voice trembling with fear. "She's a monster."

"She's your -" Sarah began to say, before realizing that she couldn't even begin to explain properly. Looking over at the door, she listened out for some hint that Hannah was on her way back, but there was nothing.

"Please," the voice stammered from the other side of the hatch, "you have to help me. He... He..."

"He doesn't want to hurt you," Sarah replied. "Just wait and..." Her voice trailed off as she realized that she had no idea what she should tell the old woman. If it was all true, if John's grandmother had really somehow survived for two decades in a tiny, dark room beneath the house, she couldn't even begin to imagine what it must have been like for her. "I can't let you out yet," she explained finally. "I'm sorry, I just can't." She turned to the door. "Hannah!" she called out. "Where are you?"

She waited.

No reply.

"Has she gone?" Scott asked.

"No, she wouldn't just leave us." Looking back down at the hatch, Sarah tried to work out what to do. She knew Hannah had said to keep the door shut, but at the same time she felt as if she couldn't leave an old woman to suffer in pain. "Just wait a little longer," she said, leaning toward the hatch. "Everything's going to be okay. We're going to get you out of there, it'll just take a few more minutes."

She waited for a reply, but after a moment she realized she could hear sobbing.

"Is she crying?" Scott asked.

"What's he done to her?" Sarah whispered. "I don't care how cruel she was to him, how could he leave her like this?" She turned to the door. "Hannah! Are you coming?"

Silence.

"She's so old," Sarah continued. "She must be ninety by now."

She paused, before stepping off the hatch and reaching down to the bolt.

"Mum, no!" Scott hissed.

"She's a sobbing old woman," Sarah replied, "and besides, she might know where John's taken Katie." She slid the bolt across. Taking hold of the handle, she slowly began to pull the hatch open, and finally she gasped as soon as she saw the frail, withered old woman at the top of the steps.

"Mum..." Scott said, taking a step back.

"Keep back" Sarah told him. "Just let me do this." Reaching down, she held out a hand. "My name is Sarah," she told the woman. "I'm John's wife."

Barely able to keep her eyes open as she looked up into the light, the old woman seemed too scared to accept the offer of help.

"Your name's Elizabeth, isn't it?" Sarah continued. "John told me that once. Please, I don't really understand what's happening here, but we can get you the help you need. Everything's going to be okay."

Still reticent, Elizabeth stared at Sarah for a moment before slowly reaching up and taking her hand. Her bones creaked as she began to climb up through the hatch, and she had to be supported as she stumbled unsteadily toward a chair. She was painfully thin, with pale skin having dried to her old bones and become almost translucent in the darkness, while her night-dress had rotted away to reveal the bare flesh beneath. There was a terrible smell coming from her, too, and most of her hair had faded away. As her whole body trembled, the old woman let out a gasp of pain when she finally reached the chair, and she still couldn't open her eyes properly.

Feeling nauseous, Scott stepped back and turned away.

"Oh my God," Sarah stammered, watching as Elizabeth struggled for breath. "This isn't possible. None of this can really be happening."

The old woman tried to say something, but

all that came from her throat was a dry, rasping gasp.

"I'll get you some water," Sarah said, hurrying to the sink and filling a glass before returning and holding it out for Elizabeth. Realizing that the old woman's hands were trembling too much, she held the glass to her lips and helped her to drink. "We have food," she continued, "but I don't know what I should give you. We're going to have to call an ambulance and get them to look at you."

"Where is he?" Elizabeth whispered as soon as she'd finished the water.

"John? He's not here right now. He's missing, I was hoping you'd know where to find him."

"Missing?" The old woman paused for a moment. Finally able to open her eyes, she stared straight ahead with milky white pupils that were freckled with blood-spots. "After everything he did... that boy... doesn't even have the courage... to face me..."

"I don't know why any of this happened," Sarah replied, with tears in her eyes, "but we're going to make it right. We're going to make sure that you get the help you need, and we're going to find John and we're going to get him to explain whatever's going on here..." Glancing at Scott for a moment, she saw the fear in her son's eyes. "I'm not going to let my family fall apart like this," she continued, turning back to Elizabeth. "I promise."

"Water," the old woman whispered. "I need more water."

"Of course."

Scott watched as his mother headed back to the sink. After a moment, he looked over at the old woman and saw that she was eying him with dark, suspicious eyes.

"You look like your father."

He stared at her, too scared to reply.

The old woman nodded. "So much like him, it's almost..."

"Katie looks like John too," Sarah said, refilling the glass. "I guess the third one'll maybe take after me."

"That same disgusting face," the old woman hissed. "Weak, pathetic, not even worthy of life."

Sarah froze, before turning to her. "What did you -"

Before she could finish, Elizabeth lunged at Scott, landing on top of him and knocking him to the ground while digging her fingernails into the edge of his face. Long and ragged, her nails sliced into his flesh and even though he tried to push her off, he couldn't help but cry out.

"Stop!" Sarah shouted, grabbing Elizabeth's arms and pulling her back. "Leave him alone!"

Panicking, she slammed the old woman into

the wall, desperate to rescue her son. Without giving Elizabeth a chance to strike again, she pushed her away and then dropped down to check on Scott, who was sobbing as blood ran down his face from the slices around his forehead and cheeks.

"It's okay," Sarah told him, taking a look at the cuts and quickly realizing that they were mostly superficial. "I'm going to get you out of here, this whole place is insane." She turned, looking for Elizabeth but seeing no sign of her.

"She fell down there," Scott whimpered, pointing toward the open hatch that led down to the basement.

Stepping over to the hatch, Sarah looked down and saw to her horror that Elizabeth's crumpled body was down at the bottom of the steps.

"I..." Pausing, Sarah realized she'd accidentally pushed the old woman to her death. "No, please..."

"Yep," Hannah said with a sigh, coming back through from the hallway, "my bag was in the bin. Can you believe that? I mean, I know John's subconscious mind probably wanted to erase any evidence that I'd been here, but..."

She stopped suddenly, watching as Sarah turned to Scott and started dabbing his wounds with a tissue.

"Were you bleeding when I left the room?" Hannah asked with a frown, before looking at the hatch. "Was that open?"

"I tried to help her," Sarah replied, still working on her son's injuries. "She attacked Scott."

"Where is she now?" Hannah muttered, hurrying to the hatch and looking down, before her eyes opened wide with shock. "Please tell me she's just taking a nap."

"I had to get her off him," Sarah stammered. "I didn't mean to push her, but she was hurting him. It was self defense!"

"No," Hannah continued, hurrying down the steps and kneeling next to Elizabeth's body. "No, this can't be happening. This is very bad." She reached out and pressed two fingers against the side of Elizabeth's neck, searching for a pulse, before feeling broken bones crunching beneath the skin. She checked the old woman's wrist, too, before sitting back.

"Is she okay?" Sarah asked, watching from the top of the steps.

"Okay?" Hannah replied, sitting back and staring at Elizabeth's body for a moment before looking up at Sarah. "Is she *okay*? No, she's not okay, her neck's broken. She's dead! She survived twenty years in the basement, and then you pushed her down the goddamn stairs!"

"It was an accident," Sarah continued, looking back at Scott and seeing that his cuts were starting to bleed again. Grabbing his shoulders, he turned him around so he couldn't see down through the hatch. "Don't look," she told him, taking another tissue from the side and dabbing at his face again. "It's going to be okay, I promise you. Everything is going to be absolutely fine, there's no need to worry. You have to believe me. Everything is going to be fine." She waited for him to show her that he understood. "Scott? You believe me, don't you?"

He nodded cautiously.

"I promise," she added, kissing his forehead. "It's going to be okay."

"This is awful and we're in a massive amount of danger," Hannah said suddenly, emerging through the hatch. "I never panic usually, but I'm panicking now. I hope you're both suitably terrified, because we have a serious problem."

Sarah turned to her.

"We need to find your husband" Hannah added. "Fast."

"He's still got Katie," Sarah replied.

"I told you not to open the hatch door," Hannah continued. "Did you not hear me say that? I was very clear and very explicit, did I somehow leave some room for doubt?"

"She was sobbing," Sarah pointed out. "I couldn't leave her down there like that, I was trying to help."

"And now she's dead, which is really bad news, not only for her but also for us."

"I swear it was an accident."

"I don't care if it was an accident or not," Hannah told her, "I care that while she was still alive, there was no ghost. Whatever else she was, she was mortal and corporeal and it was fairly easy to keep tabs on her. I was actually kind of relieved, I thought everything would be fine. I thought I was pretty much done here."

"But -"

"And now she's dead," Hannah continued, "which means that after twenty years, now she really *is* a ghost."

"Does that..." Sarah paused for a moment. "Wait, *what* did you say?"

"Now that she's finally dead, her soul has been freed and she's a ghost. And given everything that happened to her over the past few decades, I doubt she's in a very good mood. She won't be restricted to this house, either. She can go more or less anywhere, at least if there's some kind of psychological link." She looked toward the window. "She'll be able to find your husband. She'll go for him."

"What do you mean, *go* for him?"

"I mean we have to find him before it's too late," Hannah continued, turning back to her. "Come on, you have to know somewhere in this town that he might be. He wouldn't have taken your daughter if he didn't have somewhere in mind, but he definitely isn't anywhere in this house so..." She paused for a moment, as if an idea had struck her, before heading to the window and looking out.

"I don't have a clue where he might be," Sarah said, wiping more blood from Scott's face. "I think maybe it's time to call the police."

"Fat lot of good they'll do," Hannah muttered, before turning to her. "They'll only get in the way. John lived in this house with his grandmother after his mother died. Is that right?"

Sarah nodded.

"And he and his mother lived somewhere else in this town, before his mother died?"

"I'm not sure where."

"Then we'd better find out quickly," Hannah continued, "because I'm starting to get the feeling that maybe this isn't the only childhood home that John has bought recently. I think he's taken Katie to meet his mother's ghost. The problem is, now she's finally dead, his grandmother's ghost will be waiting for him."

CHAPTER TWENTY-SEVEN

Today

"I'M TIRED," KATIE WHIMPERED, as John led her along the dark garden path. "Can we go home now?"

"Soon," he replied, forcing a smile in attempt to get her to relax. "I just want to show you something first."

As they reached the front door, Katie looked up at the pitch-black house that towered above her. Compared to the house on Everley Street, this house was much taller and looked older, with a high, pointed roof and black, curtainless windows. At the same time, it was so big and so dark, and so imposing, that Katie felt as if it might topple over at any moment and crush her.

"Whose house is this?" she asked cautiously.

"It's mine now," he replied, taking some keys from his pocket. "It was my mother's, a long time ago. I lived here with her before she died. Then I had to go and live with my grandmother in that other house, but I never liked that as much." He unlocked the door and pushed it open, revealing the house's dark interior. "I was always so much happier here. Despite her faults, my mother was a good woman. She was the one who got me interested in writing, you know. She used to write stories for me, and she encouraged me to come up with my own as well. When she died..."

He paused, thinking back for a moment to the day when he'd been in his bedroom and had heard screams coming from the bathroom.

"Can we go home?" Katie asked, her eyes sore with tiredness now. "I want to go to bed."

"Soon," he told her, taking her hand and leading her across the threshold, into the dark hallway. "There's nothing to be afraid of," he added, trying the light-switch but finding it disconnected. "It's just a house. Trust me, there have been times when I've worried about ghosts in various places, but now I'm certain they don't exist. If they did, my grandmother would have started haunting me a long, long time ago. At the same time..." He paused. "I have to try one more time. Just to be sure."

"I don't like it here," Katie replied, pulling

away but unable to slip her hand out of his. "I want to go."

"Not yet." Reaching out, he swung the front door shut, shrouding the pair of them in darkness. "Don't worry," he continued, "your eyes will adjust soon. Besides, I still remember the layout of the place as if it was yesterday." He led her forward, across the hallway toward the foot of the stairs. A patch of moonlight covered the floor, shining through a window high up on the landing. "I don't even know why I bought the place," he continued. "I just decided one day that I wanted to buy all the houses where I lived when I was younger, but..."

Pausing, he turned to her.

"Tonight's the night."

"What night?" she asked.

Crouching in front of her, he looked into her tired eyes. "When my mother died, she told me that if there was any way to come back, she'd visit me. When my grandmother died, she said something similar, except that she was angry. I thought my grandmother's ghost would be haunting the house on Everley Street, but there was no sign of it. Still, I need to test it again. Even though I'm sure ghosts don't exist now, I want to see."

He turned and looked up the stairs, but there was no sign of a presence.

"I'm cold," Katie told him.

"Here." Removing his jacket, he placed it

over her shoulders. "Better?"

"I'm tired."

"Just wait a little while longer," he continued, getting to his feet. "I'll make it up to you, I promise, I just think maybe having you here will help. You look a lot like my mother, so maybe -"

Suddenly there was a faint creak from above.

"What was that?" Katie asked, her voice filled with fear.

"Nothing," he said calmly, staring at the ceiling, "or... maybe something. That's what we're here to find out."

"Daddy, I want to go!" she hissed, trying once again to pull free from his grip. "Daddy, you're hurting me!"

"Then stop struggling," he said firmly, pulling her closer. "You're just going to have to be brave for a little while longer, Katie. We all have to face our fears at some point, and there's nothing here that can hurt you. You trust me, don't you?"

"I want to go," she whimpered. "I don't like this place."

"Why not?"

Staring up the stairs, Katie paused for a moment, listening to the silence of the house. "I just don't."

"Try to put it into words. Tell me what's unsettling you."

She paused. "I feel like there's someone here," she said finally. "I don't like it."

"If there's anyone here," he replied, "it can only be my mother, and she'd never hurt anyone. I was hoping she'd be drawn to you, since you and her are so alike, and I think it might be working. Come on." He tried to lead her up the stairs, but she held back. "I think you're right. I feel a presence too. Katie -"

"No!" she said firmly.

Sighing, he reached down and scooped her up into his arms, before starting to carry her up the stairs.

"Put me down!" she shouted. "I don't want to go up there!"

"Katie -"

"Stop!"

As his daughter struggled to get free, John carried her up to the landing and then tried to set her down, only for her to pull away and try to run. Catching her just in time to keep her from tumbling down the stairs, he held her firmly and forced her around to face him in the moonlight.

"Katie," he said firmly, "I want you to listen to me."

"There's someone else here!" she shouted, with tears in her eyes. "I don't like it!"

"You have to be brave," he replied, "just for a little while longer. I need your help with this." He paused, before looking along the landing toward one of the doors. "Please, Katie," he continued, "I need you to help me, and the sooner you cooperate, the sooner we can leave. Do you understand?" Turning to her, he found that she'd stopped struggling.

"I want to go," she sobbed. "Please..."

"Come with me and let's look in the rooms," he said with a smile, taking hold of her hand again. "It's been so long since I set foot in this place, almost thirty years. I was about your age the last time. Is it hard to imagine I was so young once?"

"I don't like this house," she replied.

"And what about the house on Everley Street? Did you like that?"

She shook her head.

"I think you can sense these things," he continued. "I think you're open to them. Tell me what you felt in the house on Everley Street."

She paused. "Something angry."

"It sounds like you were sensing my grandmother's spirit," he told her. "Even if she wasn't there as a ghost, she might have been there in some other form. What about this house? What do you feel now?"

She turned and looked along the dark corridor, her eyes widening with horror as she looked at one particular door. "The same thing," she whispered, "but different. Angrier."

He shook his head. "Try again. I think you're getting confused."

"No," she replied, "I'm not. It's the same thing, but it's angrier and it feels more free, like it can get closer to us."

"If you can feel any kind of presence here at all," he told her, "it'll be my mother's. She's not angry, Katie, I promise, you're just a little mixed up." Still holding her hand, he began to lead her along the dark landing. "Let me show you my old bedroom, it might help you to see things better."

"I don't want to," she whimpered, trying to hold him back.

"We all have to do things we don't want to do sometimes," he replied, as they approached one of the doors and he pushed it open, revealing a dark, empty room. "Sometimes we have to leave a place we don't want to leave, or a person we don't want to leave. Sometimes we have to be brave when we want to run. Do you think you can be brave for me tonight, Katie?"

Turning, she looked toward the door at the far end of the landing. She knew something was in there, waiting for them, but she was scared to tell he father in case he decided to go and look.

"This was my room," he said, leading her through to the bare room. "What do you think?"

Still looking over her shoulder, Katie kept her eyes fixed on the farthest door.

"It wasn't very fancy," John continued, "but it was home. Before my mother died, I was happy here, even after my father left. My mother was troubled, she'd been damaged when she was younger by my grandmother, but she was devoted to me and she did everything she could to look after me. I understood that, even back then, and in return I did my best to help her. Even when she started to get sad, she refused to slow down, and then..." He paused for a moment. "She used to write stories for me, Katie. Wonderful, fun stories. I wish I still had them, I wish I could read them to you, but my grandmother burned them all." Letting go of her hand, he made his way to the far corner of the room. "My bed was right here. She used to sit on the end and read to me."

Katie was still staring at the far door, terrified by the idea that she might have to go closer. As her father continued to talk about his childhood, she stepped back onto the landing, and a moment later she realized she could hear a faint sobbing sound coming from one of the other rooms. She flinched, her body filling with tension, before taking one more step back until she could see into the bathroom.

She was shocked to see that the light was on, and a middle-aged woman was curled up on the floor, crying as her whole body trembled.

Katie opened her mouth to call for her

father.

Suddenly a second woman walked past the first, crossing the doorway too quickly for her face to be seen.

Shocked by what she was witnessing, Katie simply stared in horror.

"You're weak," a shrill, angry female voice hissed from the bathroom. "You're a disgrace, and you're raising a weak son. It's obscene."

"Please," the woman on the floor sobbed, "just go. Just leave us alone."

"You want to be a martyr, is that it?" the angry woman asked, stepping back into view. With her back to the door, she reached down and grabbed the sobbing woman's face, forcing her to look up. "I've read those stories you write. They're nothing but self-absorbed lies."

"Please..."

"I won't let you make my grandson weak," the angry woman continued. "You might be a complete failure, but at least he still has a chance. You've threatened to kill yourself so many times, but you're too much of a coward to go through with it. Well, here. Let me help you."

"No!" the other woman shouted, but it was too late. The angry woman forced a green bottle to her lips and tipped the contents into her mouth, holding her firmly as she fought back. After a few gulps, the sobbing woman began to scream, but still the contents of the bottle flowed into her mouth until she fell back, clutching her throat.

"I don't know what you're making such a fuss about," the angry woman sneered. "This is what you wanted, isn't it?"

Crying out, the sobbing woman leaned forward as blood flowed from her mouth. She was screaming louder than ever now, and clawing at her own belly as if she was trying to get the liquid out.

"Just a few more minutes," the angry woman explained, standing over her. "I'll call an ambulance soon and say I found you like this. I'll take Jonathan in and raise him properly. He'd have had no chance with you. I don't know why you turned out so badly, there must have been something wrong with you."

Suddenly, the door swung shut and the screaming stopped.

Katie blinked, before hearing footsteps nearby. Turning, she saw her father emerging from the other room, apparently oblivious to everything that his daughter had seen.

"Are you okay?" he asked, putting a hand on Katie's shoulder. "Are you picking up on anything yet?"

Turning to look back at the bathroom door, Katie felt her whole body stating to shake with fear.

"What is it?" John asked. "Katie, talk to me, are you -"

Before he could finish, there was a firm,

hard bump against the inside of the far door. He turned and looked along the landing, seeing the door in the gloom.

"Daddy," Katie whispered, squeezing his hand tight, "can we go now?"

"There's nothing to be scared of," he told her.

"I don't like this house. I just saw..." Her voice trailed off, and she was too scared to say the words.

"What did you see?"

"I'll tell you when we're outside," she whispered, with tears in her eyes. "I just want to leave right now."

"This house is fine. The other house, the house on Everley Street, that's the one that's scary."

"No, they're both scary."

"Just stay calm," he reminded her, even though he couldn't take his eyes off the distant door. "If there's a ghost here, it's a friendly one. Trust me, I know. You have to -"

Suddenly there was another bump, louder this time, as if something on the other side of the far door was trying to get their attention.

"I..." John began to say, before his voice trailed off. Still staring at the door, he was starting to sense that something was wrong.

"Daddy," Katie whispered, with tears in her eyes, "what's in the basement at the other house?"

He turned to her, his eyes filled with shock. "What do you mean?"

"There's something down there. What is it?"

"There's nothing in the basement," he replied. "Katie, you -"

Stopping suddenly, he realized that maybe she was right. He couldn't remember clearly, but he had a sudden sense that there *was* something in the basement of the other house. He'd spent so much time worrying about the room where his grandmother had died, he'd allowed those concerns to overshadow the deep, gut feeling that the real presence was in the basement, behind the breeze-block wall that had just appeared one day as if from nowhere. For a moment, he found himself remembering slivers of things that had happened down there: Alison laughing as she forced her way past and headed down; Hannah insisting on taking a look; his father pulling a loose block away; and finally, he remembered carrying the breeze-blocks down from the garden, almost as if he himself had built the wall.

Katie gasped as the far door began to creak open.

"Daddy," she hissed. "I want to go!"

"Wait," he replied, his mind racing as he remembered more and more. It was as if he had two entirely separate minds, and now the barrier between them was breaking down, allowing memories to flood through. "Katie -"

Before he could finish, an unseen force grabbed the little girl and pulled her away, slamming her into the wall and then dragging her across the landing as she screamed for help. Reaching out for her, John tried and failed to grab her hand before racing after her. After just a few paces, however, he heard a rattling sound nearby, and he turned just in time to see something slamming into his face, hitting him on the temple and knocking him out cold.

Still screaming, Katie tried to dig her fingers into the floorboards, but she was powerless to keep herself from being dragged along the landing and through the far doorway, into the darkest room in the house. A figure was waiting, reaching down to grab the little girl's shoulders as the door swung shut.

CHAPTER TWENTY-EIGHT

Today

"NO," JOHN REPLIED, trying not to sound frustrated as he stood in the hallway with the phone against one side of his face, "I already told you, her funeral is being held in Essex. That's what she wanted. It's tomorrow."

"Oh dear," Dorothy Ormerey replied on the other end of the line, "that doesn't leave much time to organize flowers, but I shall certainly try. What's the name of the -"

"There's no point," he said firmly.

"I beg your pardon?"

"I really don't have time to talk about this right now," he continued, on the verge of telling the nosy old woman to go to hell. He felt angrier than usual, more combative, and he didn't have time to explain everything to people. "Don't send flowers. If you want to do something for her, make a donation to charity. Any charity'll do."

"So who exactly is going to the funeral?" she asked.

He paused, trying to think of a few names he could throw at her. "People in Essex," he said finally. "No-one you know."

"I see."

He could almost hear the frown over the line.

"Well," Mrs. Ormerey continued, "if that's what she really wanted..."

"It is."

"And I suppose -"

"I really have to go," he added, "so I'm sorry I could be more help. I'm sure my grandmother would have appreciated the fact that you called, though."

"So which -"

Before she could ask another question, he put the phone down and then, for good measure, he disconnected it from the wall. The past few days had been filled with old women calling up to ask the same goddamn things, and he was sick of dealing with them. Was it so hard for them to understand that his grandmother had wanted to be buried back in the area where she'd grown up? He hadn't even been lying, not about the most important part: his grandmother *had* been born in Essex, and even though she'd never expressed any desire to be buried there, he felt it was a believable story, so people should just shut up and believe it.

Heading back to the kitchen, he stopped for a moment, feeling as if the world was spinning all around him. He'd been working hard all morning, but there was still so much to do. He made his way to the hatch and then down into the basement, where he'd already set up several lights that meant he could see what he was doing. At the basement's far end, he'd already laid his grandmother's body out on a table, and he'd used ropes to tie her down. After all, although he'd been certain earlier in the day that she was dead, there had been a few twitches and clicks from her body that had left him a little worried. He'd considered calling an ambulance, but he was worried they might take her away and make her better, and then bring her back again, and then everything would start again.

He wanted to be free, which meant getting rid of her as fast as possible.

Halfway across the basement, he'd begun to build the wall, using breeze-blocks he'd pulled from behind the greenhouse. He'd done some research at the local library and he'd managed to mix together a thick gray paste that seemed to be holding the blocks firmly in place, and after working methodically for several hours he'd been able to build part of a wall that even he found impressive. Reaching down, he grabbed another of the heavy blocks and carried it over, before putting it in place on a layer of paste he'd been smoothing out when the phone rang a few minutes ago. He figured it would take the best part of a whole day to finish the wall, but that didn't matter. All that mattered was getting his grandmother out of sight and -

Suddenly he heard a faint gasp. Looking toward the table, he saw no sign of movement, and he told himself that dead bodies had a habit of releasing trapped air. A moment later, however, he heard another gasp, and this time he thought he saw, in the gloom, his grandmother's face moving slightly.

"No," he whispered, his eyes wide with shock, "you're dead. You have to be."

He got back to work on the wall, hoisting block after block into place. He didn't really have a plan for after the wall was in place, but he figured he'd come up with something. There were a few more gasps from the table, but he was able to ignore those and focus exclusively on the task at hand, and once the wall extended three-quarters of the way across the basement he stepped back for a moment and admired his handiwork. Having never done anything remotely like building a wall before, he'd worked carefully and methodically, and he felt that he'd done a surprisingly good job. All that remained was to get it finished and -

Suddenly his grandmother let out a faint moan, and this time there could be no doubt: he turned and looked at her, and he saw to his horror that she was trembling slightly, causing the ropes around her torso to start rubbing against her nightdress.

He froze for a moment, before telling himself that he was simply imagining the whole thing. Reaching down, he grabbed another breezeblock and put it in place, working faster this time and starting to become a little sloppy. Ignoring the continued moans from the table, he grabbed another block, but this time he fumbled as he put it in place. The block slipped from his hands and fell, landing on the front of his foot and causing him to cry out in pain. He pulled his foot free and limped back, feeling a growing sense of discomfort around the area of his big toe. Still, he figured he could examine the damage later. For now, as his grandmother continued to moan, he ignored the pain and pulled the breeze-block up, this time sliding it quickly and firmly into place.

"Jonathan," a voice whispered suddenly, its tones slurred and barely understandable, "what are you doing?"

He froze, trying to convince himself that his imagination was running out of control.

"I..." the voice continued. "Jonathan... I..."

Slowly, he turned and looked over at her, and he saw that his grandmother had turned to look at him. Her face seemed distorted somehow, as if one side was almost melted, and he knew enough about medical situations to realize that she'd most likely suffered a massive stroke.

"If you don't..." she hissed, struggling to speak, "let me... up... I swear I'll kill you... just... like..."

Staring at her, he shook his head.

"You're just like your... mother..." she whispered.

Reaching down, he picked up another breeze-block and for a moment he considered going over to the table and crushing the old woman's skull. His hands were trembling, but he knew deep down that he could never do anything so direct. It would be better to simply hide his grandmother away and pretend she was gone forever, so he put the breeze-block in place and began to add more paste. He figured she'd waste away quickly enough.

"No," she hissed, trying to raise he voice but unable to get above a pained, slurred whisper. "No! Somebody help me!"

Grabbing one of the rags he'd brought down to cover the floor, John hurried to the table and placed the fabric firmly over the old woman's mouth, quickly tying a gag that rendered her cries virtually inaudible. To make doubly sure that no-one would hear her, he put another rag in place, and then another, before stepping back and watching as she struggled in vain. She could clearly only use one side of her body, with the stroke having paralyzed the rest, and he figured that she'd probably just die fairly quickly if he left her alone. When he'd found her on the bedroom floor, he'd been certain she was already dead, and he'd had time to get used to the idea. The thought of going back to how things used to be, of returning to that hopeless life, was too horrifying to contemplate.

Ignoring her continued attempts to get free, he went back and got to work finishing the wall.

***

"You're becoming quite the regular visitor, aren't you?" said the woman behind the library counter as she looked at the books he was checking out. "It's good to see people taking literature seriously."

He smiled politely, but really he was just waiting for her to scan his books so he could leave.

"Sound-proofing for the home studio," the woman read from the first book's cover. "Are you a musician?"

"I..." He paused. "No. I mean, it's something I'm thinking about for the future."

"Caring for stroke victims," she continued,

looking at the second book. "Oh, has someone in your family suffered a stroke?"

"No," he told her, "I just... I thought it'd be good to read up on something like that. You never know when you might come across someone who's hurt. I mean, if you did the wrong thing, you might end up accidentally killing someone them." He stared at the book, watching as the woman scanned it and then stamped the plate on the inside of the front cover. "Better to be safe than sorry," he continued, "right?"

***

"It's okay," he said a few days later, as he finally finished installing the third layer of insulation that he hoped would stifle any sounds his grandmother made, "it'll be over soon. This is just to avoid any unfortunate accidents."

Whereas the breeze-block wall had ended up as a surprisingly professional-looking job, the sound-proofing hadn't gone so well, but he figured it wouldn't be necessary for too long. Looking over at the table, he realized his grandmother had barely moved all day, even though he could tell she was still alive. He'd given her no food and no water, preferring to let nature take its course, but now he knew that the final moment had come. The room was ready to be sealed, which meant he had to say goodbye.

Stepping over to the table, he looked down at her gagged, tired face.

"Can you hear me?" he asked.

He waited.

Silence.

"Hey." He nudged her shoulder, and this time she opened her eyes. "I'm going now," he told her. "I know you probably think I'm evil, but after everything you did to me..." His voice trailed off for a moment, but he figured there was no point going through it all again. The old woman undoubtedly remembered all the beatings to which she'd subjected him, all his screams, all the punishments he'd endured, everything she'd done to him, but now the misery belonged in the past. "This is just how it has to be," he continued, turning and heading toward the small gap in the breeze-block wall.

He stopped suddenly as he heard a faint, muffled groan. Turning, he saw she was tugging at the ropes with weak arms, but he was confident she wouldn't be able to get off the table, and her voice had been so badly damaged by the stroke, she could barely even whisper.

Hearing a scratching sound nearby, he looked down and saw a couple of rats scurrying out of a hole in the wall, just next to a damp patch. For a moment, he worried that the rats might start gnawing on his grandmother's flesh, but he quickly forced such ideas out of his mind and instead slipped through the gap before pushing the final breeze-block into place. He had to work hard to keep his mind blank, and to block out all the thoughts that were racing through his head, but finally he finished setting the last block and he stood back.

The wall was complete.

It was tempting to try to imagine what was happening on the other side, to think about his grandmother tied down and alone in the cold, dark space, with only rats for company. At the same time, he knew he'd only end up losing his mind if he dwelt for too long on such matters, so he took a deep breath and forced himself to think about other, happier things. It wasn't easy to switch his thoughts, but he figured he'd get better with practice. Once he was certain that there were no sounds escaping from the hidden room, he switched off the lights and carried them up into the kitchen before putting them neatly away. After a moment, he looked down at the floor and imagined his grandmother below, but he quickly reminded himself that he shouldn't think about her. Instead, he got to work on other chores, and to his surprise he found that he could quite easily keep his mind from dwelling on the morning's events.

And then, with no warning, he heard someone knocking on the door. He froze, uncertain as to whether or not he should answer, but a moment later there was another knock. Making his way cautiously to the hallway, he looked through and saw a pale shape on the other side of the frosted glass, with a hint of red in the center. Whoever it was, it definitely wasn't a policeman, and he figured he couldn't hide forever. After taking a deep breath, he made his way over.

"Hey," Alison said with a smile, as soon as John opened the door. She was wearing a cream sweater with a big ladybird on the front. "Long time, stranger."

Startled, he stared at her for a moment. He'd spent the morning tidying the house, lost in his own thoughts... or at least that was what he told himself. For a moment, he felt as if maybe there was something he'd forgotten, as if his mind had divided into two completely separate halves, but that sensation passed quickly enough. Instead, he focused on the surprise of seeing Alison standing in front of him. After all, she was one of his few friends, or at least she had been, back when he still *had* friends, back in his school days.

"Are you gonna invite me in?" she asked, raising a skeptical eyebrow, "or do I have to force my way through the door? Which, to be fair, wouldn't be so easy after my recent op." She looked down at his foot. "Are you limping?"

"Oh, it's nothing," he replied. "I just hurt my

toe when..." Pausing, he realized he didn't remember how he'd hurt it. "It's nothing. Come in."

CHAPTER TWENTY-NINE

Today

"NO, REGINALD, IT'S OKAY," Hannah said, with the phone against the side of her face as she led Sarah and Scott across the dark street, "we've found it just fine. Thanks for your help."

Cutting the call, she passed the phone back to Sarah, while staring up at the dark house that towered above them.

"Now *this* looks more like a haunted house," she said with a faint smile, admiring the bay windows and the high, pointed ceiling. After a moment, she turned to Sarah again. "Don't you think so? The house on Everley Street just seems a little modern and boring, but this one, this one I can really see having a few ghosts. All we're really missing is some thunder and lightning, maybe some atmospheric rain..."

"Are you sure this is the place?" Sarah asked, staring up at the house with a hint of fear in her eyes.

"John bought this place three years ago," Hannah explained. "That's what his lawyer says, anyway. Did he never mention it to you?"

"It's starting to look like there's a lot he never mentioned to me."

"It seems he's been planning this little spree for a while," Hannah continued, "buying up the houses where he lived as a child. And this place..." She paused for a moment. "From birth to the age of nine, Jonathan Myers lived in this house with his mother. And then she died one night, supposedly after drinking a bottle of bleach, and he went to live with his grandmother."

"Do you really think he's here right now?" Sarah continued.

"I think there's a very, *very* good chance."

"Stay here," Sarah told Hannah. "Keep an eye on Scott."

"No way."

"I'm serious!"

"So am I!" Hannah replied. "I'm not the one who stays outside where it's safe, I'm the one who goes inside and sorts things out."

"My daughter might be in there!"

"And I'll bring her out," Hannah said firmly, before making her way up the steps toward the dark front door. "Trust me, this is what I do, it's my job. I fix deaths that have gone wrong."

"Are Dad and Katie really in there?" Scott asked, looking up at his mother.

"I don't know, honey," she whispered.

"We have to go inside," he continued. "We have to save Katie."

"Save her?" Sarah paused. "We have to *find* her first, but I don't think -"

"Come on," Scott said firmly, taking her by the hand and leading her after Hannah, who was already at the door.

"You have to stay behind me," Sarah told her son, "and do exactly what I tell you at all times, is that understood? I'm not going to let you argue with me here. This is just how it's going to be."

"The door's unlocked," Hannah muttered, gently pushing against the handle and causing the door to slowly swing open. "Still think no-one has come this way in the past few hours?"

"John!" Sarah shouted, pushing past her and hurrying into the dark hallway. "Katie!"

"No reply," Hannah continued, stepping over to join her and looking up toward the top of the stairs. "Either they left, or..."

"Or what?" Sarah asked.

Hannah turned to her. "Or this is the part

where you wait down here and I go up to fix everything."

"But -"

"You have to stay behind me," Hannah continued, "and do exactly what I tell you at all times, is that understood? Seriously, you can't argue with me here, that's just how it's going to be."

"That's exactly what *you* said to *me*," Scott said, nudging his mother's arm.

"Is my husband really insane?" Sarah asked, looking around for a moment before turning back to Hannah. "Please, tell me this is all some kind of joke."

"It's all some kind of joke," Hannah said flatly. "Oh, wait, no, that's a big stinking lie. Sorry."

"He's not like this," Sarah continued. "He's a good person, an honest person, he'd never hurt anyone!"

"Of course not," Hannah replied, heading to the stairs and starting to make her way up to the landing. "The everyday John Myers wouldn't hurt a fly, because he put all his hatred and rage into a second version of himself, and it's *that* version that does things like walling his granny up in the basement. Kind of efficient, really. You almost have to respect him."

"Do you think Katie's okay?" Scott whispered to Sarah as they followed Hannah upstairs.

"I'm sure she's fine," Sarah replied, her voice filled with tension. "Your father wouldn't let anything happen to her. We're just overreacting."

"Empty landing," Hannah said, looking both ways for a moment before heading off to the left, "with all the doors open except for one at the far end. If you ask me -"

Stopping suddenly, she looked at one of the doors. Pushing it open, she looked into the dark bathroom. "This is where it happened," she muttered.

"Where what happened?" Sarah asked.

For a moment, Hannah watched as she saw a dark shape on the floor, and in the back of her mind she heard a loud scream.

"This is where John's grandmother murdered his mother," she whispered, "and made it look like suicide."

Sarah stared at her. "No. That's not possible."

"Elizabeth was one twisted old woman," Hannah continued. "She expected great things of her daughter, and when she realized she wasn't shaping up, she decided to get rid of her and start again, this time with John. She threw her own daughter away like a doll." She paused, before pulling the door shut. Turning, she spotted John's unconscious body on the floor, just inside one of the nearby doors. Hurrying over, she dropped to her knees before checking for a pulse and then gently nudging the side of his face.

"John!" Sarah called out, hurrying over and kneeling on the other side of her husband. "John, are you okay? Where's Katie?"

"He's not responding," Hannah muttered, nudging his face again. "Either he's been knocked out, or he's entered some kind of psychological breakdown phase." She paused, before slapping the side of his face as hard as she could manage. "Wake up!" she yelled.

Gasping, John opened his eyes.

"Excellent," Hannah continued, "he was just knocked out."

"Katie!" John stammered, sitting up and looking around.

"We know everything," Sarah told him. "About your grandmother, about the basement..."

"What about Katie?" he asked, before getting to his feet and looking out into the corridor, where he saw Scott staring at him. "Where is she?"

"Isn't she with you?" Sarah asked.

"She was, but -" Slowly, he turned and looked toward the closed door at the far end of the landing.

"She's in there," Hannah said firmly, stepping past him and staring at the door for a moment. "And she's not alone."

John paused. "What do you -"

"I've got some bad news for you," Hannah continued, turning to him. "This might come as a shock, but I'm afraid your grandmother is dead."

He frowned.

"Really dead this time," she added, "not fake dead, not dead as in just bricked up in the basement of the house on Everley Street. She's really, finally dead, and that means she's really, finally dangerous because now she actually *is* a ghost, and now..." She paused, before turning back to look at the closed door. "I'm not excusing anything you did, John, but your grandmother was bad when she was alive and she's worse now. She murdered your mother, for one thing, but then I've got a feeling that you suspected that. After all, you heard the screams from your bedroom when you were a boy."

"Wait," he replied, "how do you know all of this? You're just..." His voice trailed off for a moment.

"Just what?" she asked, stepping toward the door.

"Well, you're just some girl I met at a cafe and then at a book club."

"Cute," she whispered, turning and pressing her right ear against the door. "I'm way more than just some girl you met at a cafe. To start with, I came here specifically to sort this mess out, and then there's also the fact that I -"

Before she could finish, she heard a loud

bumping sound. The door shuddered and she took a step back.

"What the hell was that?" Sarah asked, before hurrying forward. "Katie!"

"Don't!" Hannah said firmly, reaching out and putting a hand on Sarah's chest, to hold her back. "This is a very delicate situation and you really need to leave it to me."

"My daughter -"

"Will be fine, if you just do what I say and leave it to me." Hannah stared at the door for a moment, before reaching down and turning the handle. "You all might want to look away right now," she continued. "Either that, or get very good, very fast, at not screaming."

She paused, before nudging the door and causing it to slowly creak open, revealing the dark room beyond. In the center of the room, barely visible in the low light, Katie was sitting on a chair with her eyes closed.

"Katie!" Sarah shouted, rushing forward before Hannah once again held her back. "Let me get to her!"

"Not yet," Hannah said firmly.

"Why not? She's just sitting there!"

"She's not just sitting there."

"What..." Sarah paused, looking around at the darkness. "What do you mean? There's no-one else here!"

"Can't you see John's grandmother?" Hannah asked, her eyes widening with horror. "That's good, because I can see her and trust me, it's not a pretty sight."

Stepping forward, she kept her eyes fixed on the scene ahead. While the others could only see Katie on the chair, Hannah could see that old woman sitting right next to her, with her arms around the trembling child and one hand on her neck, holding her tenderly but with a hint of menace..

"What's going on in there?" John asked, joining Sarah in the doorway. "What's wrong with her?"

"Just wait," Sarah told him.

"But -"

Grabbing his arm, Sarah forced him to stay back. "Trust Hannah."

Approaching the chair, Hannah looked more closely at Elizabeth's withered hand, which was holding Katie's neck tightly. She paused for a moment, seeing the fear in the little girl's eyes.

"It's okay, Katie," she said finally with a faint, forced smile. "I'm here to put things right."

Katie was staring at her, but tears were running down her cheeks and her whole body was shaking. After a moment, however, she glanced up at Elizabeth before closing her eyes.

"You can see her too, can't you?" Hannah

continued. "That's why you've got your eyes closed. That's good, that's smart. Just keep them like that and I'll see what I can do here, okay?" Crouching in front of the chair, she looked up at Elizabeth's face and saw dark eyes filled with pure hatred. "Hello, Elizabeth," she said after a moment. "I'm here to help you, because I've got a feeling you're a little lost right now. It's not much fun being newly dead, is it?"

"They're all useless," Elizabeth whispered, staring at the little girl's face. "Just a waste of breath."

"You've got your voice back," Hannah replied. "I guess that's one plus point."

"I don't know what's wrong with them. I did my best, I raised them to be good, strong people, and they just became disasters, the lot of them. Pathetic weaklings."

"You don't really think that, do you?"

"My own daughter was an idiot," Elizabeth continued. "I couldn't even beat an ounce of sense into her. You have no idea how hard I worked to make her better, but it was a waste of my time. I had to put her out of her misery in the end, but I thought at least I had a chance to get that boy Jonathan on the right path, but he was even worse. Weak-willed and spineless, that's his problem. He never understood that I was just trying to toughen him up."

"By punching him?" Hannah asked. "By stubbing out cigarettes on his back? By telling him he was worthless and by fracturing his soul so badly that he had to become two people?"

"Excuses."

"Maybe." Hannah paused. "You don't want to hurt Katie, though, do you? She's your great-granddaughter. What did she ever do to upset you?"

"She's like him," Elizabeth hissed, squeezing the girl's throat a little tighter. "They're all just a disgrace to the family name."

"But if -"

"He left me down there to die!" the old woman continued, turning to Hannah. Her eyes were black as night, leaking dark tears that ran down her ravaged face. "I didn't die, though. I refused. I found a way. I ate rats and I drank filthy water that leaked through the ceiling. I couldn't speak when I was alive, the stroke robbed me of that, and I was too weak to even get anyone to hear me, but I *refused* to die. That boy has to pay for what he did to me."

"You're dead," Hannah replied. "You don't get to decide who pays for what."

"Don't you dare tell me what I can and can't do," Elizabeth hissed, squeezing Katie's throat again, causing the girl to let out a pained gasp. "You don't know anything! You don't even -"

"I know why your daughter really died,"

Hannah said firmly, interrupting her. "John's mother. I know she didn't really drink bleach to kill herself. I know you forced it down her throat -"

"No!"

"I was there."

Elizabeth paused, her features flickering with memories of that moment.

"I was there," Hannah explained. "There are rules about intervening, so I couldn't do anything to stop you. Nowadays things would be different, I don't stick to the rules so much anymore, but back then... Back then I just sat in the corner and sobbed as I watch what you were doing."

"You're a dirty liar!" Elizabeth hissed.

"Am I?" As if to prove her point, a scream erupted from the corner of the room. Hannah and Elizabeth both turned to see two spectral forms shimmering in the dark: Elizabeth, a little younger than when she'd died, pouring a bottle into the mouth of a sobbing middle-aged woman. It was the same scene that Katie had witnessed earlier in the bathroom. "We both know I'm not lying," Hannah continued, watching with stony-faced anger as the scene briefly played out, before the two spectral figures faded. She turned back to Elizabeth. "You murdered your own daughter."

"I put her out of her misery," Elizabeth whispered, looking down at Katie's terrified face.

"You gave up on her," Hannah continued.

"You decided she wasn't good enough, so you wanted to get rid of her and start again with her son, except he wasn't good enough either, was he? You warped his mind and you'd have killed him too if that stroke hadn't interrupted. And now what, is Katie the third try? Maybe you should just accept that none of these children can live up to your impossible standards. Your long, bitter life is over, Elizabeth. All that's left now is for you to go into the light and see what's waiting for you on the other side."

"Leave me alone," she hissed, causing Katie to gasp again as she began to crush her throat.

"You're holding her very tightly," Hannah replied, watching as Katie struggled for breath. "You're actually causing several bones in her neck to bend slightly. Any more pressure, and they'll start to break. Is that what you want?"

"I want one of these children to live up to my expectations," Elizabeth replied, squeezing harder. "I want them to stop being so weak!"

"No," Hannah said firmly, reaching out and grabbing the old woman's hands. "You don't get to do that. Children aren't projects you can toss away if they don't work out the way you wanted." Taking hold of Elizabeth's hands, she began to peel the old woman's fingers back one by one, forcing her to let go of Katie's throat. "You're dead Elizabeth," she hissed, "and that's a big problem for you, because it means you're in my realm now, and you can't bully me. You're going exactly where I want you to go, and the more you try to fight back, the more you annoy me. Is that something you really want to do? Are you so stupid, so utterly idiotic, that you're going to annoy me on purpose? Because let me tell you, you're already well along that particular path."

"Go to hell," Elizabeth growled, turning to her.

"Funny," Hannah replied, "I was about to say the same thing to you."

Without giving Elizabeth a chance to react, Hannah grabbed Katie's shoulder and pulled the girl away, knocking her to the floor and then shoving her toward Sarah and John.

"Bring her back!" Elizabeth shouted, getting up from the chair and rushing toward the door. "She's mine!"

Suddenly able to see the horrific figure, Sarah grabbed Katie and pulled her out of the way just in time.

"Get out of here!" Hannah shouted, scrambling to her feet and hurrying over to join them. "I'll deal with everything, but you have to get your children out of this house! It's the children she wants!"

Grabbing Scott, Sarah began to lead the children to the stairs, before looking back and seeing that John was staring in horror at Elizabeth.

"It'll be okay!" Hannah shouted at her. "Just go! If you -"

Before she could finish, Katie screamed. Turning, Hannah saw that Elizabeth was standing in the doorway, her gaze fixed firmly on John.

"Come on," Sarah said, scooping Katie up into her arms and carrying her down the stairs, with John hurrying after them. "I can't let you see this."

"You're all grown up," Elizabeth hissed, stepping toward John. "Maybe you're not as pathetic as I thought."

John stepped back until he was next to the bannister.

"It's okay," Hannah told him, "I'm going to get rid of her. This can't be allowed to continue."

"Is it true?" John asked, staring at his grandmother. "Did you kill my mother?"

"I gave her life," Elizabeth replied, stepping closer.

"And then you took it away," he continued. "Everyone believed that she'd killed herself. You told me she was weak and I actually believed you! I heard her screaming!"

"She should have poured that bleach down her throat much sooner," Elizabeth told him. "She threatened to do it so many times, I just helped her to get the job done efficiently."

"Was it worth it?" Hannah asked, edging closer to them. "All the pain, all the screams? Then again, maybe it was easy for you. It's not as if John's mother was the first person you ever killed. I know about all the others, Elizabeth. All the people in your life who didn't live up to your expectations, so you ended *their* lives too. Your first and second husbands, your sister when you were both just little girls, even your own father. You went through your whole life like this, getting rid of people whenever you decided they weren't good enough. I wasn't able to stop you while you were alive, but now you're dead, you're in my world."

"If only one of them had been good enough," Elizabeth hissed, reaching a hand out toward John's face. "Just one, that's all I asked. One decent human being out of them all."

"You told me she killed herself," John said with tears in her eyes. "You lied about everything."

"I thought it might toughen you up," Elizabeth replied, "but I suppose that was a hopeless case. Still, I can always try again with your daughter."

Before John could reply, his grandmother lunged at him, knocking him back and breaking through the old wooden bannister, sending the pair of them crashing over the edge. Hannah called out and ran forward, but all she could do was watch in horror as John fell down onto the floor below. Racing down the stairs, she found him on his back as his grandmother's ghost stood over him.

"I won't leave this family alone," the old woman hissed, "until I finally -"

"No," Hannah said firmly, stepping over to her. "You're going to leave everyone alone."

As Elizabeth began to scream, Hannah placed her hand over the old woman's face and forced her down. Elizabeth's eyes were burning now as Hannah's fingers dug deeper, and a kind of cold blue flame was starting to ripple across the old woman's body, consuming her from within. The scream grew louder and more pained, but Hannah didn't even flinch as she stared down at her, and finally a vast white light seemed to open up in Elizabeth's chest, flaring briefly and then sparking through the air until finally Hannah was left alone, with her hand still outstretched as ribbons of fire danced across her fingers.

"When I said go to hell," Hannah whispered darkly, "I meant it."

Turning, she saw that John wasn't moving. She got down onto her knees and checked his pulse, before staring at his face for a moment. Hearing footsteps nearby, she turned to see Sarah in the doorway.

"You'd better call an ambulance," Hannah told her. "And while it's on its way, you might want to think about how you're going to explain all of this, because I think people might have a few questions."

CHAPTER THIRTY

Today

"IS SHE GONE?" Sarah asked as she sat in the hospital corridor, her eyes red and sore from all the tears. After a moment, she turned to Hannah. "I mean, is she *really* gone?"

"She's really gone," Hannah replied.

"But she was already dead," Sarah continued. "Doesn't that mean she could come back? If I hear a bump in the night or a scratching sound, how do I know it's not her?"

"Because I personally supervised her journey to the next life," Hannah continued. "Trust me, there's no coming back from where she went."

Hearing footsteps nearby, Sarah looked up, only for a doctor to hurry past without even acknowledging her. "They're not telling me anything," she muttered with frustration. "Why aren't they telling me anything? John's father said he'd pay for the best care, but no-one's saying a damn thing!"

"It's going to take them a while to work out what to do with him," Hannah replied. "I doubt they've had too many people like him before. Elizabeth really did a number on him, she tore his soul in two when he was a boy."

"So the man I married was..." Sarah paused, trying to understand the enormity of what had happened. "He was, what, only half a man?"

"The good half. The human mind is a powerful thing. Sometimes the damage is too extreme, it spreads and destroys the whole mind, but some people find a way to compartmentalize that damage and split it off into a separate mind. That's what John did, except that his damaged half took control whenever he thought Elizabeth's ghost might be around. The good side of John genuinely believed his grandmother had died all those years ago, and the damaged side tried to protect him and maintain that fiction. It was a symbiotic relationship. Kind of cool really, apart from the context."

Sarah paused for a moment. "I'm not ever going to get him back, am I?"

"I think you will," Hannah told her. "In

time."

"But how could people not have realized Elizabeth was still alive?" Sarah asked. "How could people have lived in that house without realizing that an old woman was sealed-up in the basement, living off rats and rainwater for twenty years?"

"Like I said, the human mind is a powerful thing. People would have sensed that something was wrong, but fear would take over and kept them from investigating. They'd put it out of their thoughts. Of course, it helped that Elizabeth lost her voice in the stroke, and that she was barely strong enough to move. John's sound-proofing attempts were completely useless, but that didn't matter because Elizabeth couldn't make much of a sound at all. Still, people living in that house will have sensed her, and that's why they thought the place was haunted. It was a kind of referred fear, but on a grander scale. Children are less able to deceive themselves, though. They're more aware."

"It still seems hard to believe," Sarah told her.

"Well, that's the thing when I show up," Hannah replied, getting to her feet and putting her hands in her pockets. "Thousands of people die every day on this planet, and the vast majority of those cases slip past without causing a problem. I'm only assigned the cases where strange, unlikely or improbable things are happening, and this one definitely qualifies."

"You're *assigned* cases?" Sarah asked. "By who?"

"By my boss."

"And who's that?"

"Someone who thinks people should suffer a little less than they do."

"But -"

"And I'm not going to give you a straight answer," Hannah added, interrupting her. "You can ask until you're blue in the face, but I'll just keep on being enigmatic and mysterious."

Sarah stared at her for a moment. "Who are you?"

Hannah smiled.

"Really, I mean," Sarah continued. "You seem to know so much about all of this, but... Who are you?"

"Do you want coffee or tea from the machine?" Hannah asked.

"Tea, but -"

"Then that's who I am," Hannah continued. "I'm the person who's going to go and get you some tea. And I'm pretty sure that within the next few minutes, a doctor is going to come out of the door at the end of the corridor, he's going to be wearing a pink tie of all things and he's going to tell you the treatment plan for John. And at least then you'll have some idea for how things will improve, and they *will* improve. Slowly, but it'll happen. The human mind is capable of recovering from almost anything, given the right help."

"But -"

"Tea," Hannah added, turning and heading around the corner. "I'll get that tea."

"Please be okay," Sarah whispered, looking down at her hands for a moment. All she could think about was John, and the way that her husband's entire life and mind seemed to have unraveled in just a few days once he'd gone back to the house on Everley Street. She wanted to believe Hannah, to believe that there might be a chance of things getting back to normal, but at that exact moment she felt as if the whole world was crashing down onto her shoulders.

"Mrs. Myers?"

Looking up, she saw a nurse standing next to her, holding a cup of tea.

"Here," the nurse continued, handing the tea to her. "Someone asked me to give this to you."

Taking the tea, Sarah got to her feet and headed to the corner. Looking along toward the machine, she realized there was no sign of Hannah. After a moment, she turned to the nurse.

"The person who asked you to give this to me... Did she leave a message?"

"Sorry," the nurse replied, "she just said you needed tea. Oh, and -" She held out her hand, passing a pile of crumpled pieces of paper to her. "She also said to give you these, and ask you to pass them on to your husband. She said she saved them years ago and that maybe he'd like them."

"Thank you," Sarah replied with a frown. As the nurse walked away, she set the cup of tea down and began to look through the pieces of paper, which turned out to contain some kind of handwritten story. She didn't recognize the writing, although it looked a little like John's while also seeming subtly different. The pages seemed to be out of order, and finally she found the first, which contained an underlined title. "The Curse of the Beast in the Shed: A Novel," she read out loud, "by..." She paused, feeling a faint shiver pass through her chest as she realized she recognized the name. "Rachel Myers. John's mother?"

"Mrs. Myers?"

Hearing another voice, she turned, just in time to see a doctor making his way toward her from the door at the far end of the corridor. She couldn't help but notice that he was wearing a pink tie.

***

"You have got to be kidding," the first medical examiner said as he and a couple of colleagues worked on one of the skeletons that had been found in the basement, with lights mounted on stands all around. "Twenty years? No way, that's impossible."

"I know," the second examiner replied, "but that's actually what happened. I didn't believe it at first either, but I checked the files and it's all in there. Crazy, huh?"

As they continued to work, neither of them noticed Hannah in the corner, watching them.

"Looks like a scoliosis patient," the first examiner said as he carefully laid a section of spine onto a sheet, complete with a metal rod screwed into several of the vertebrae. "So the guy was, what, feeding people to his dead grandmother?"

"The doctors reckon his subconscious mind was taking over and doing these things," the second examiner muttered. "Whenever there was a chance of his secret being discovered, he switched into a mode where he'd do anything to keep it hidden. I guess some people are just messed up and can't be saved. Goddamn psycho probably had no idea he was even -"

Hannah kicked a rock, sending it skittering toward the two examiners.

"What the hell was that?" the first examiner asked, looking at the rock and then turning to look toward Hannah, still not seeing her.

"What's wrong?" his colleague asked. "Worried about ghosts?"

"In a place like this? No kidding, man!"

"Let's just get on with the job. There's no such things as ghosts."

They got back to work, but a moment later Hannah kicked another rock toward them.

"This place is freaking me out," the first examiner said. "I just want to get the hell out of here."

"Fine, but don't get flaky on me. There's probably just a lot of rats down here, they probably move stuff as they scurry through the shadows."

"Thanks. That makes me a feel a lot better."

"It's better than ghosts, right? Face it, at least rats actually exist. Ghosts don't."

"Of course not," Hannah whispered with a faint smile, before kicking another rock toward them, this time freaking them out even more and sending them hurrying back up the steps.

EPILOGUE

One year later

"WHEN CAN DADDY COME HOME?" Scott asked as he climbed out of the car and pushed the door shut. "He seemed a little bit today, more like he used to be."

"The doctor says he needs to stay there for a while longer," Sarah replied, opening the boot and pulling out grocery bags. "It's looking better than before, though. They'll start by letting him come home for day visits, maybe for weekends, and then they'll take it from there."

"But he'll be okay in the end, won't he?" Scott continued, grabbing two of the bags and heading toward the house. "He's not going to be there forever, right?"

"No, not forever," Sarah replied, slamming the boot once the final bag was out. "Just until he's okay again."

"Do you really think he'll get better?" Katie asked, with a hint of fear in her voice. "Every time we go and see him, Scott says he thinks he seems better, but I don't think he's right. I don't think he seems different at all."

"The truth is somewhere in the middle," Sarah told her. "He's getting better slowly, but he might never be completely well. It's just a matter of taking small steps each day and hoping that eventually..." She paused for a moment, seeing the concern in her daughter's eyes. "Whatever happens, it'll be okay. Your father has problems, they went undiagnosed for years, but they've been recognized now and you might not see it, but he's making real progress."

Katie frowned.

"Now take these bags inside," Sarah continued, "and I'll start thinking about dinner."

As Katie headed into the house, Sarah leaned into the car and grabbed her bag. As she locked the doors and prepared to go inside, however, she heard footsteps getting closer, and she turned to see a smart, twenty-something guy approaching. Well-dressed and with a kind smile, the guy seemed a little hesitant.

"Can I help you?" she asked.

"Sarah Myers?"

If you're a journalist," she replied, instantly becoming defensive, "I really don't think I can help you. My husband's health is a private matter -"

"I'm not a journalist," he said, holding his hands up in mock surrender, "I promise. I'm not here to dig into his personal details, I'm a researcher."

"I'm still not sure I can help you," she continued, glancing at the house to make sure the children were inside, before turning back to him. Over the past year, she'd dealt with scores of journalists, and they never quite seemed to give up digging into the story. "We're dealing with things privately."

"My name is Daniel," the guy told her as they shook hands. "I was very sorry to hear about what happened to your husband, I hope your children are okay."

"They're just fine," she said cautiously.

"And you? The whole experience must have been extremely harrowing."

"I'm fine too."

"That's great." He paused, as if he was a little nervous about continuing. "I'm actually here to ask you about Hannah."

"Hannah?" Pausing, Sarah felt relieved and uneasy at the same time. In all the drama surrounding the events a year ago, the presence of

Hannah had been one thing she'd kept very much to herself. After all, she had no idea how to answer the inevitable awkward questions. "Listen, I really have no -"

"I know you know who I mean," he added, interrupting her.

She paused again. "What did you say you were researching again?"

"I guess you could say I'm researching Hannah herself," he continued. "I'm sure I don't need to tell you that she's... elusive. Something of an enigma."

"I really don't think I can help you..."

"I think you can," he replied, before smiling. "I'm sorry, that must have come across wrong, but... The truth is, I've been researching Hannah for a while now. Digging into the story, following leads, tracking down people who might have come across her. It's not easy, people tend to not talk about her much, some people even seem to doubt she exists, but I *know* she does." He paused. "I also know she was involved in what happened with your husband last year."

"I haven't seen her since then."

"I know that too. She's not exactly famous for sticking around. She never has been."

"I don't know anything about her," Sarah continued. "Not really. I don't know how to get in touch with her, if that's what you want. Hell, I don't even know her surname or where she comes from."

"I figured. Everyone basically says the same thing. She turns up like a whirlwind, she does whatever she needs to do, and then she gets out of town real fast."

"So you understand that I can't help you?" she replied. "There's literally nothing more than I can tell you."

He paused for a moment, before nodding. "Okay," he said finally. "Okay, I get that. To be honest, I'm kind of used to people saying things like that. I guess Hannah isn't the kind of person who stops to chat about herself much."

"She definitely isn't," Sarah replied. "Listen, I don't mean to be rude, but I have to get inside and make dinner for my kids. I wish you well, I really do, and I'm sorry I can't help you, but... Good luck."

"Thanks," he said, taking a step back. "I've got a feeling I'm going to need it."

"And if you happen to bump into her some time," Sarah continued, "could you give her a message for me? Could you tell her... Thanks. Just thank her for me again, okay?"

"Will do."

"She really helped my family," Sarah added. "Tell her John really appreciated the copy of his mother's novel, too. I think it really helped him and..." She paused, realizing she'd probably said too much. "Well, I hope you track her down eventually."

Turning, she headed along the driveway. The sudden appearance of some guy asking about Hannah seemed a little odd, and his questions had reignited some thoughts she'd managed to avoid for the best part of a year. Reaching out to grab the door handle, she couldn't help but wonder who Hannah had really been, and where she was now.

"Mrs. Myers?"

Turning, she saw that Daniel had followed her and was now standing just a few feet away, still smiling.

"I'm sorry," she told him, feeling a little unnerved, "like I said, I can't -"

"I know what you said," he replied, interrupting her as his smile began to fade, "but the thing is, I'm afraid I'm going to have to insist."

She froze for a moment. "Listen -"

Before she could finish, he grabbed her by the shoulders and pulled her back, before pushing her forward again and sending her crashing through the window next to the door. Landing hard on the hallway floor, her skin torn by broken glass and with more pieces falling all around her, she let out a gasp as she tried to get up, only to find that the impact had broken or fractured her hip.

"Mummy?" Katie shouted, as she and Scott raced through from the kitchen.

"Run!" Sarah screamed, as she heard the

door being broken down. "Get help!" Turning, she saw Daniel stepping calmly into the hallway, and after a moment he reached down, grabbed her by the collar, and hauled her up until their faces were just inches apart.

"Like I said," he said firmly, as his pupils expanded to reveal a hint of speckled red and yellow coloring in the center, "I really must *insist* that you tell me everything you know about Hannah."

BOOKS IN THE
DEATH HERSELF SERIES

Alice Isn't Well
The House on Everley Street
The Dead Ones
Harper's Hotel Ghost Girl (coming soon)

AMY CROSS

Also by Amy Cross

The Soul Auction

"I saw a woman on the beach. I watched her face a demon."

Thirty years after her mother's death, Alice Ashcroft is drawn back to the coastal English town of Curridge. Somebody in Curridge has been reviewing Alice's novels online, and in those reviews there have been tantalizing hints at a hidden truth. A truth that seems to be linked to her dead mother.

"Thirty years ago, there was a soul auction."

Once she reaches Curridge, Alice finds strange things happening all around her. Something attacks her car. A figure watches her on the beach at night. And when she tries to find the person who has been reviewing her books, she makes a horrific discovery.

What really happened to Alice's mother thirty years ago? Who was she talking to, just moments before dropping dead on the beach? What caused a huge rockfall that nearly tore a nearby cliff-face in half? And what sinister presence is lurking in the grounds of the local church?

Also by Amy Cross

Darper Danver: The Complete First Series

Five years ago, three friends went to a remote cabin in the woods and tried to contact the spirit of a long-dead soldier. They thought they could control whatever happened next. They were wrong...

Newly released from prison, Cassie Briggs returns to Fort Powell, determined to get her life back on track. Soon, however, she begins to suspect that an ancient evil still lurks in the nearby cabin. Was the mysterious Darper Danver really destroyed all those years ago, or does her spirit still linger, waiting for a chance to return?

As Cassie and her ex-boyfriend Fisher are finally forced to face the truth about what happened in the cabin, they realize that Darper isn't ready to let go of their lives just yet. Meanwhile, a vengeful woman plots revenge for her brother's murder, and a New York ghost writer arrives in town to uncover the truth. Before long, strange carvings begin to appear around town and blood starts to flow once again.

Also by Amy Cross

The Ghost of Molly Holt

"Molly Holt is dead. There's nothing to fear in this house."

When three teenagers set out to explore an abandoned house in the middle of a forest, they think they've found the location where the infamous Molly Holt video was filmed.

They've found much more than that...

Tim doesn't believe in ghosts, but he has a crush on a girl who does. That's why he ends up taking her out to the house, and it's also why he lets her take his only flashlight. But as they explore the house together, Tim and Becky start to realize that something else might be lurking in the shadows.

Something that, ten years ago, suffered unimaginable pain.

Something that won't rest until a terrible wrong has been put right.

Also by Amy Cross

American Coven

He kidnapped three women and held them in his basement. He thought they couldn't fight back. He was wrong...

Snatched from the street near her home, Holly Carter is taken to a rural house and thrown down into a stone basement. She meets two other women who have also been kidnapped, and soon Holly learns about the horrific rituals that take place in the house. Eventually, she's called upstairs to take her place in the ice bath.

As her nightmare continues, however, Holly learns about a mysterious power that exists in the basement, and which the three women might be able to harness. When they finally manage to get through the metal door, however, the women have no idea that their fight for freedom is going to stretch out for more than a decade, or that it will culminate in a final, devastating demonstration of their new-found powers.

Also by Amy Cross

The Ash House

Why would anyone ever return to a haunted house?

For Diane Mercer the answer is simple. She's dying of cancer, and she wants to know once and for all whether ghosts are real.

Heading home with her young son, Diane is determined to find out whether the stories are real. After all, everyone else claimed to see and hear strange things in the house over the years. Everyone except Diane had some kind of experience in the house, or in the little ash house in the yard.

As Diane explores the house where she grew up, however, her son is exploring the yard and the forest. And while his mother might be struggling to come to terms with her own impending death, Daniel Mercer is puzzled by fleeting appearances of a strange little girl who seems drawn to the ash house, and by strange, rasping coughs that he keeps hearing at night.

The Ash House is a horror novel about a woman who desperately wants to know what will happen to her when she dies, and about a boy who uncovers the shocking truth about a young girl's murder.

Also by Amy Cross

Haunted

Twenty years ago, the ghost of a dead little girl drove
Sheriff Michael Blaine to his death.

Now, that same ghost is coming for his daughter.

Returning to the small town where she grew up, Alex
Roberts is determined to live a normal, quiet life. For the
residents of Railham, however, she's an unwelcome
reminder of the town's darkest hour.

Twenty years ago, nine-year-old Mo Garvey was found
brutally murdered in a nearby forest. Everyone thinks
that Alex's father was responsible, but if the killer was
brought to justice, why is the ghost of Mo Garvey still
after revenge?

And how far will the real killer go to protect his secret,
when Alex starts getting closer to the truth?

Haunted is a horror novel about a woman who has to
face her past, about a town that would rather forget, and
about a little girl who refuses to let death stand in her
way.

Also by Amy Cross

The Ghosts of Hexley Airport

Ten years ago, more than two hundred people died in a horrific plane crash at Hexley Airport.

Today, some say their ghosts still haunt the terminal building.

When she starts her new job at the airport, working a night shift as part of the security team, Casey assumes the stories about the place can't be true. Even when she has a strange encounter in a deserted part of the departure hall, she's certain that ghosts aren't real.

Soon, however, she's forced to face the truth. Not only is there something haunting the airport's buildings and tarmac, but a sinister force is working behind the scenes to replicate the circumstances of the original accident. And as a snowstorm moves in, Hexley Airport looks set to witness yet another disaster.

Also by Amy Cross

The Girl Who Never Came Back

Twenty years ago, Charlotte Abernathy vanished while playing near her family's house. Despite a frantic search, no trace of her was found until a year later, when the little girl turned up on the doorstep with no memory of where she'd been.

Today, Charlotte has put her mysterious ordeal behind her, even though she's never learned where she was during that missing year. However, when her eight-year-old niece vanishes in similar circumstances, a fully-grown Charlotte is forced to make a fresh attempt to uncover the truth.

Originally published in 2013, the fully revised and updated version of *The Girl Who Never Came Back* tells the harrowing story of a woman who thought she could forget her past, and of a little girl caught in the tangled web of a dark family secret.

Also by Amy Cross

**The Devil, the Witch and the Whore
(The Deal book 1)**

"Leave the forest alone. Whatever's out there, just let it be. Don't make it angry."

When a horrific discovery is made at the edge of town, Sheriff James Kopperud realizes the answers he seeks might be waiting beyond in the vast forest. But everybody in the town of Deal knows that there's something out there in the forest, something that should never be disturbed. A deal was made long ago, a deal that was supposed to keep the town safe. And if he insists on investigating the murder of a local girl, James is going to have to break that deal and head out into the wilderness.

Meanwhile, James has no idea that his estranged daughter Ramsey has returned to town. Ramsey is running from something, and she thinks she can find safety in the vast tunnel system that runs beneath the forest. Before long, however, Ramsey finds herself coming face to face with creatures that hide in the shadows. One of these creatures is known as the devil, and another is known as the witch. They're both waiting for the whore to arrive, but for very different reasons. And soon Ramsey is offered a terrible deal, one that could save or destroy the entire town, and maybe even the world.

Also by Amy Cross

Asylum
(The Asylum Trilogy book 1)

"No-one ever leaves Lakehurst. The staff, the patients, the ghosts... Once you're here, you're stuck forever."

After shooting her little brother dead, Annie Radford is sent to Lakehurst psychiatric hospital for assessment. Hearing voices in her head, Annie is forced to undergo experimental new treatments devised by a mysterious old man who lives in the hospital's attic. It soon becomes clear that the hospital's staff, led by the vicious Nurse Winter, are hiding something horrific at Lakehurst.

As Annie struggles to survive the hospital, she learns more about Nurse Winter's own story. Once a promising young medical student, Kirsten Winter also heard voices in her head. Voices that traveled a long way to reach her. Voices that have a plan of their own. Voices that will stop at nothing to get what they want.

What kind of signals are being transmitted from the basement of the hospital? Who is the old man in the attic? Why are living human brains kept in jars? And what is the dark secret that lurks at the heart of the hospital?

Also by Amy Cross

The Devil's Hand

"I felt it last night! I was all alone, and suddenly a hand touched my shoulder!"

The year is 1943. Beacon's Ash is a private, remote school in the North of England, and all its pupils are fallen girls. Pregnant and unmarried, they have been sent away by their families. For Ivy Jones, a young girl who arrived at the school several months earlier, Beacon's Ash is a nightmare, and her fears are strengthened when one of her classmates is killed in mysterious circumstances.

Has the ghost of Abigail Cartwright returned to the school? Who or what is responsible for the hand that touches the girls' shoulders in the dead of night? And is the school's headmaster Jeremiah Kane just a madman who seeks to cause misery, or is he in fact on the trail of the Devil himself? Soon ghosts are stalking the dark corridors, and Ivy realizes she has to face the evil that lurks in the school's shadows.

The Devil's Hand is a horror novel about a girl who seeks the truth about her friend's death, and about a madman who believes the Devil stalks the school's corridors in the run-up to Christmas.

AMY CROSS

For more information, visit:

www. amycross.com

AMY CROSS

Printed in Great Britain
by Amazon